YOU ARE MY

hope

WILLOW WINTERS

Mason gave me chills when I first laid eyes on him. The good kind. The kind that make your body ache, and your heart hammer.

It's not fair that his touch eased my pain.
That his lips on mine made my worries vanish.
That his love gave me a reason to breathe again.

With him I felt complete, as if fate had given me a second chance.

Then I learned the truth—the sins and secrets of what had really brought us together.
I only hope we can go back. I never could have imagined this.

This is book 2 in the You Are Mine duet.
You Are My Reason should be read first.

Kintsukuroi,
Means to repair with gold.
The once destroyed and shattered,
Repaired with binds to hold.

The bits are mended over time,
The piece stronger than before.
It's more beautiful for being broken.
Different? Yes, but ruined no more.

YOU ARE MY

hope

prologue

Mason

One month ago

DON'T LET THEM SEE.

Her words echo in my head as I stalk toward the quiet bedroom. She whispered them against my lips last night. The cool air slipped between us as she broke our heated kiss and slowly opened her eyes in the dark of night.

The streetlamp shined down around us like a spotlight on the back porch of her place on the Upper East Side. The city life slept quietly so late at night—or early in the morning, depending on how you look at it. Only the sinners like us were left awake.

Don't let them see. She left me with the parting plea and here I am... complying with her wish.

I've never crept through anyone's back door before. Not once in my life have I had to sneak around like this.

I don't want to keep this up, but here I am. What the hell has this woman done to me? *I'm wrapped around her little finger.*

She doesn't want anyone to notice me walking through her door because she's ashamed. I know that's why she doesn't want people to know we're together.

This isn't a fling; this isn't a rebound fuck. There's something more to us now, but she still doesn't want the world to know.

The floorboards creak under my weight and I hesitate in the doorway, the dim lamp from the hall filling the dark room with a hint of light. I'm being careful so her neighbors won't be able to hear anything. I just don't want to disturb her.

It's obvious she's sleeping, but then she stirs beneath the silk duvet until finally she opens her eyes and sees me. She tilts her head to the side as she looks at me, burying her cheek into the pillow, a soft smile playing on her lips as she utters a pleasant feminine hum.

"I missed you," she whispers and her voice is laced with an equal mix of sleep and lust.

If only she knew the real reason I crave her touch. The reason I'm so tempted to break all my rules.

"I'm sorry I'm late," I tell her in a deep, rough voice as I start unbuttoning my shirt. A smirk lifts up the corners of my lips as her eyes sparkle with humor. She doesn't care when I come and go, so long as I lie in her bed at night, or she in mine.

Her doe eyes peer back at me while I slip off my button-up and let it pool into a puddle at my feet. I yank my tight white undershirt over my head and look back to see those lush lips parted.

My muscles ripple as I let the tank drop to the floor, the moonlight bathing the room and the two of us in a faint glow.

She may want to keep this a secret but she wants me nonetheless, and she can't hide it. I've become addicted to the way she looks at me like she needs my touch to stay grounded, just as she needs to breathe air to survive. I'm conditioned to crave the faint sounds of her quickened breath as she waits for me to come to her. *As if she'd die without me.*

I'm slow to unbuckle my belt as my eyes roam down her luscious curves. She's mine to take. Mine to touch. *Mine to keep.*

I don't want to sneak around anymore and I don't give a shit who knows. I'm tired of all the secrets and politics, all the gossip in this town.

The anger boils in my blood as I grip my leather belt tighter, making it sing in the air as I pull it through the loops. The buckle drops to the floor with a *thunk*. All the while my gaze is on her gorgeous eyes, and she stares back at me with the same desire I have for her.

The past is over and done. No one else will ever know what really happened—not her, not anyone. *So why can't I truly have her?*

"Mason." She practically whimpers my name and it pulls the beast in me closer to her. My knee dips into the bed, making it groan with my weight as I crawl over to her.

Her soft blue eyes pierce through me, cutting through the dark room. More of the soft lighting from the city slips between us as the heat kicks on and the curtains sway. The way the light kisses her skin as she pushes away the blush silk duvet makes her all the more beautiful.

She's laid out for me. *All for me.* She needs me.

I crush my lips to hers and dig my fingers into the flesh of her hips as she spreads her thighs for me. Her soft moans fill the hot air between us.

She's ashamed to be moving on so quickly. Especially with a man like me. I wasn't made for a woman like her. I'm someone who could tarnish her sterling reputation and make the cracks in her picture-perfect life even deeper. To say I'm rough around the edges is putting it lightly, but I have what it takes to keep her.

She thinks she's ruined, but she's perfect. It's my sins and secrets that could destroy us both. I'll never let them come to light. Not now that I have something worth fighting for.

CHAPTER

one

Julia

Present day

I'M CAUGHT BETWEEN MY NEED TO RUN AWAY AND the need to know the truth. I need the truth from him. No more secrets; no more lies.

He promised.

He loves me.

There's just no way.

"Did you do it?" The question leaves me in a single weak breath and in an instant, something snaps into place. It's as if he's not at all shocked by what I'm saying. As if he's been waiting for this.

No. My body turns to ice; my blood freezes in my veins and I can't believe this is reality. It can't be true.

Mason takes a step forward, starting to move around the island and it breaks me from my denial.

It's my cue to run, a natural instinct that takes over. The stool falls hard, crashing to the floor as I take off, but Mason's faster, grabbing my waist and jerking me backward. I cry out from fear and he releases me, only for me to fall onto the tiles at my feet. His large frame towers over me, and he puts his hands up as though he's approaching a wild animal. I feel like I am just that. Eyes wide as I stare up at him, my heart pounds painfully in my chest. *Thump, thump, thump.*

"Did I do what?" he asks with a coldness I haven't seen before and his eyes narrowed. This isn't the man I know.

My bottom lip trembles, the small bit of strength I had vanishing as I take in the raw truth. "Did you kill my husband?"

The words leave me in agony as they hover in the tense air between us.

I can't believe I even asked him that. *Deny it. Please deny it. Tell me I'm a fool. And this, whatever this is, it's something that's already over and never happened.*

Mason stands up straight, giving me enough space so that my breath can come back to me, but my lungs refuse to fill until he answers me.

"They think they can do whatever they want," Mason says, still standing over me as he snatches the paper from where it lays on the floor. I didn't even realize I'd dropped it.

No. That's not what he should be saying right now.

"Your husband wasn't a good man," Mason adds lowly,

his eyes piercing me before flicking back to the paper. He crumples it in his fist as a cold sweat spreads across my skin.

"No." It's all I can say. "You didn't." I try to say more but it's in vain as my throat dries up and constricts. I don't know if it's the shock or if I'm just that pathetic. I didn't fall for a murderer. Mason couldn't—

"I did." Mason's confession makes me light-headed, and a sickness churns in my gut.

My heart twists with a pain that's unbearable as I crawl away quickly, trying to escape. I slip against the ground, crashing hard to the cold, unforgiving floor.

"No!" I scream at him, leaving a strangled cry to linger between us. It's only then that I even register I'm crying.

I try again to run, managing to get to my feet this time and the foyer is so close as I stumble out of the kitchen. I call out for help, although I doubt anyone could hear us. Not here inside Mason's home. I practically slam into the front door, but Mason's right behind me.

With one hand on the door and one on the knob, his hard body presses against mine, trapping me between him and my only escape.

His large body cages me in. I'm left facing the door, barely able to stand or breathe. "You were never supposed to know," he whispers. I shrink beneath him, the weight of the reality crashing down on me. "I'm sorry."

I've fallen in love with my husband's killer. I've slept with him and given him everything.

"I'm not going to hurt you, Jules." His warm breath sends shivers down my back as he adds, "But I can't let you leave."

CHAPTER
two

Julia

THE ONLY THING YOU NEED TO WORRY ABOUT IS remembering my name. Just my name and what I've done to you tonight.

Mason whispered those words so close to my ear, sending a shiver of want through my body. It was everything I desired when I met him. He made that promise to me the first night, and I so easily fell into his bed.

I'd been so desperate to feel *anything* but the heartache and misery I'd succumbed to.

If only I could take it back.

If only I'd known this man was the cause of my pain.

Anger seethes inside me as I stare at him across the

other side of his bedroom, where he's sitting in the corner. His elbows rest on his thighs as he hunches over the edge of the reading chair with his head in his hands. His fingers run back and forth along the back of his head as if there's a thought inside his mind he can't quite reach.

He won't look at me; he merely stares at the ground in complete silence. All the while I'm shattered, and with every minute that passes I feel the broken pieces more and more.

My body is restless and my eyes burn with a desperate need to cry, but I have nothing left.

I try to scoot my exhausted body up the bed to soothe my sore arms, but the rope tied around my wrists tightens with the sudden pull, chafing me. I wince and suck in a breath through clenched teeth; my shoulders are screaming in pain.

Hours have passed since I found out the truth. Hours spent restrained to this bed. When I wouldn't stop scream-ing and fighting him, clawing at him and trying to escape his strong grip, he tied me up.

It's been only minutes since he's come back into the room, though. Minutes since he's opened that door and let his eyes rest on me. I'm pathetic, weak and completely at his mercy. Captive to a man I loved who hid a secret so dark and corrupt it's ruined me. I'll never be the same. There's no way to recover.

Ticktock. Ticktock.

It's only been minutes since he lowered himself into the chair without speaking a word to me, I remind myself. He sits in a chair I brought from my home to his. A chair I'd cried countless tears in after my husband died.

And yet he says nothing. It's the silence that kills me.

"I hate you." The words slowly scrape their way up my

sore throat. They're barely audible, since my voice is so raspy and weak from all the screaming.

He slowly lifts his head, his corded muscles rippling. For the first time since I've been with Mason, after months spent falling in love with him, I feel real agony. The small involuntary shudder my body makes proves there's a bit of fear present too.

The sharp lines of his jaw look more intense in the dim light, the shadows only making them seem more severe. His steel gray eyes are like daggers as he captures my gaze.

I can't breathe; I can't look away. I hate him for what he did then and I hate him for how he's making me feel now.

"You don't," he says and his voice is rough and deep. He sounds stronger than before. But it's a lie. All lies.

I do. I hate him more than I could ever express.

Finally, I gasp for air rather than crying any more tears, breaking his gaze to stare up at the ceiling. Even that minor movement makes the raw wounds at my wrists hurt. I try to hide it, though.

I gave this man everything. How could I have been so foolish? "I hate you more than you'll ever know," I murmur to the ceiling in an eerily calm voice although my heart is anything but.

The creaking of the floorboards grabs my attention, and my gaze whips to Mason as he stands. Goosebumps spread slowly over every inch of my skin as he rises.

His muscular frame seems so much larger in this moment, and a hint of a lethal concoction gives a low stir in the pit of my stomach. He's always been dominating and intimidating, but this is something darker… something more.

I have nothing to protect me, not even a sheet. He

stripped the linens off the bed before tying me up and I was left in only the underwear and baggy, thin cotton T-shirt I slipped on this morning. The chill is getting to me.

The bed dips and groans as he places a knee on it only inches away from me. I would struggle to pull away, but I'm stuck here. Both of us know that.

"I love you, Jules," he murmurs and his words are a mix of strangled pain and determination. He's a broken man with a tortured soul.

I don't know how I could possibly look at a man who's done this to me and feel any kind of sorrow for him, but I do.

I've met men before who've been wound tight, waiting to go off like a bomb. They were always constantly on edge and ready for a fight at a moment's notice. Mason's not like that. Instead he's like thread loosely wrapped around a spindle, nothing but a mess of tangles. It's not soft string; this thread's sharp to the touch and there's no hope at unraveling it without cutting yourself.

I never knew how deeply he'd wounded me. I had no idea that while I was busy mending myself and leaning on him for support, he was watching me bleed out, saying nothing. The closer he got, the deeper the inevitable betrayal, but that didn't stop him. He had so many chances to tell me what he'd done.

I let my head drop to look him in the eyes. It makes my heart swell with an unbearable pain to have him so close to me. To see how injured he is, but knowing it's nothing compared to what he's done to me.

I truly loved him. I thought fate had given me a second chance at love and happiness. I knew it was too good to be true.

"How could you do that?" The aching question isn't what

I'd planned to say when I narrowed my eyes. "You're sick," I add and the words are gritted out somehow, bearing the strength I was aiming for and I wait for him to strike back with the same venom I've given him.

His steady breathing is somehow calming and it irritates me as I watch his chest rise and fall. "Maybe," he says before rising off the bed and turning away from me. My heart plummets at the sight of his back to me and my expression crumples. It physically hurts me to know he's hurting too. I thought I knew agony before. My God.

Why did this happen? How could it happen?

Tears threaten and I shove them back, hating all of this and praying to just wake up and find it's merely a bad dream. *Please! Please, I would give anything for this to only be a nightmare.* My silent prayers are disrupted by the wood floors creaking as Mason heads toward the door, leaving me here and not giving me any indication of what's to come.

"Aren't you going to say you're sorry?" I whisper the ragged question. Maybe that's what's most shocking; he hasn't said he's sorry. Not for tying me up and keeping me here… not for murdering my husband almost a year ago.

His tall frame pauses in the partially opened doorway, stopping in his tracks as he registers what I've said. He turns his head slowly to look back at me over his shoulder, his hand still on the carved glass doorknob.

"I already told you that I'm sorry. You were never supposed to know the truth."

"You're only sorry that I found out?" I ask with equal amounts of disbelief and hurt.

His eyes dart to the floor and the bedroom door groans as it opens slightly wider.

He glances up at me hesitantly, as if debating on telling me something. It would be the truth; I can see it, can feel the intensity. Instead he says nothing, walking out of the bedroom with even strides before slamming the door shut behind him.

CHAPTER
three

Mason

The past is dark,
And filled with pain.
Mistakes were made,
And nothing gained.

If I had known,
I'd have found a way.
But what's done is done,
The past never goes away.

OMEONE KNOWS. THE KNOWLEDGE BRINGS A chill that prickles down my shoulders to the base of my spine. Someone knows what I've done. It's been nearly a year. So much time has passed and yet they've said and done nothing until now. All the possibilities of who it could possibly be are jumbled in the forefront of my mind. For hours I've been focused on this rather than what I've done to Jules. My poor Jules.

I didn't think anyone knew until Jules received that letter.

It destroys me that I couldn't lie to her. I couldn't hide what I'd done. Some sick, twisted part of me is relieved that now she knows.

But then I see the way she looks at me. I deserve the hate… I knew it would come to this and still I want to fix it. I don't have any other choice but to make this right. I can't let her go.

I won't.

They say if you love someone, you should let them go.

That's bullshit.

I didn't know it until I lost her, but I had nothing to live for without Jules. There's no possibility in this life that I'm going back to what I was before her.

The idea that she could turn me in has barely even registered. It's merely a passing thought that intrudes upon the images replaying in my head of seeing her walk away from me. The memories of her pushing against my chest, violently scratching and kicking me. Her screams that she hates me echo in my ears over and over.

She doesn't mean it. She can't hate me. Not for that.

I swallow thickly as I descend the stairs, gripping the

railing and matching the pounding of my heart with the heavy thud of my bare feet.

I can make it right. I can and I will. My palm is clammy as I hold the railing tighter.

It's a priority to figure out how to make her forget the past and remember her future is with me. I nod, envisioning how this was *supposed* to be. How it could have ended so beautifully.

I check to make sure the front door's locked as I pass the foyer, still completely trashed from our earlier struggle and head for the dining room, ignoring the mess.

More importantly, I need to find out who the fuck knows what I did and if they have any evidence. That's first. Jules needs time to cool off and while she does, I need to work out who sent that letter and why.

Jules is angry, and I get that. Saying it was a shock is obviously an understatement. I flick on the light and my eyes are instantly drawn to the bar. To a vice I desperately need to lean on while I process my lack of grace at what I did to her.

She was never meant to find out what happened. I was a different man then. If I'd known her at the time, I would have handled it differently. I would have ripped her away from that piece of shit and taken her for myself. In another life, perhaps it happened that way.

But that's not our reality.

Picking up a glass from the rack on the edge of the bar, I remember the haunting look in her eyes; the glass clinks as the adrenaline in my blood begins to wane for the first time since seeing her face as she read the letter.

I don't know how to fix this. Every other trouble Jules has had has been easy to remedy. This... I know it's unforgivable, but what she wants isn't an option for us. I can't go back to what I once had and who I used to be.

I need her and she may not want to admit it right now, but she needs me. Deep down, she knows it's true. This doesn't change anything.

She just needs time and so do I. I'll figure out a way to keep her and make her happy again. *It's not the first time I've destroyed her,* I think as the bottom of the heavy glass hits the bar top.

I crack my neck to the side as I hear her cry out again, sharp profanity echoing down the stairway and hall. Her voice is raw and hoarse, and I know the regret plagues her.

A smirk lifts up my lips. She's right, I must be sick. The thought that lingers is that she has to regret moving in with me. My house is on the edges of the city and in a secluded, remote location. If we were at her place, the neighbors would have heard everything, and the cops would have already been called. I'd be fucked.

I give a small grin as I twist off the cap to the whiskey and slowly pour it into the tumbler. No one can hear her but me while we're in here.

I'm the only knight in shining armor she's going to get.

I bring the glass to my lips and the smile vanishes, my eyes drifting to the lit fireplace. She turned it on earlier, claiming it brings a warmth to the darkness in the dining room.

Downing my whiskey and then raking my fingers through my hair, I let out a frustrated sigh over the sound of her screaming.

She's going to be sore and angry, and the marks on her wrists will need time to fade, but she'll survive. She'll get over it.

Whoever wrote that note though, whoever tried to tear my sweetheart from me, that fucker won't survive this. I grit my teeth as I slam the glass down and feel the burn of the liquor spread through my chest.

The thought prompts me to head to the entryway. The rug is crooked from when I dragged Jules up the stairs, and the lamp on the hall table is on its side, but at least it's not broken. My keys and wallet are still on the floor from when she knocked them off the table in her frantic attempt to hold on to something, anything to keep her from being taken upstairs.

My eyes dart up to the wall behind the iron banister. A low hum of admonishment leaves me as I bend down to pick up the scattered items.

The dents and scrapes on the walls are going to be a bit more difficult to fix. Recalling the feel of her struggling against me stirs an unrecognizable emotion inside my gut. I close my eyes and picture how I held her tight against me, forcing her still and pushing her against the wall, trapping her. She never stopped fighting, though. I count every little mark. Her nails scratched against the drywall, desperate for something to save her. It's *evidence* that's not so easy to clean up.

I did what I had to do, I think although the justification sounds hollow in the back of my mind.

The keys jingle as I toss them onto the table, scooting it back into place and then I snatch up the crumpled piece of thick cream parchment.

The note that destroyed what I had.

I clear my throat, willing the images and memories to go away as my chest tightens with unbearable pain. I had her. I had my sweetheart and she loved me, I know she did.

The letter crinkles as I focus my eyes on it and turn my back to the staircase, resting my shoulder against the doorframe of the dining room and listening to the crackling of the fire.

It's handwritten and leans more toward feminine penmanship. My eyes narrow as I look over every inch of the paper attempting to recognize the curve of a letter, something, anything. Not a damn memory comes to mind. There's no name. No way to identify who it came from.

Dear Julia,

It pains me to tell you this, but I can't stand to watch from a distance as you fall into a trap. Your husband was murdered. I know this is going to shock you, but I have proof. You may not believe me, but I pray that you do.

Mason Thatcher murdered him. Don't trust him. Don't let him know that you know. If he finds out, you won't be safe.

All I can tell you is that you need to run. Stay far away.

I can't say any more. I hope this letter finds you safe and you take every word for what it is, the truth.

Truly yours,

X

Proof. My narrowed gaze focuses on the single word, my heart racing faster and faster. There's not a single possibility that someone has proof.

There were no cameras around. There's no fucking way anyone saw. Her prick of a husband was leaving his apartment after screwing his mistress, and on his way back home. Back to Jules, his wife he didn't deserve. My chest rumbles with a low murmur of anger at the memory. His arrogance was one of the things I hated most about him.

My eyes whip to the stairs as I hear Jules call out again. Her voice is cracked and so uneven I can't make out a damn word she's saying. I grit my teeth and resist the urge to burn the note. I need it and the envelope it came in.

This is a fucking mess. But I make a solemn promise to Jules: I'll fix this.

Gripping the banister, I wait a moment for her cries to cease and then slowly ascend the staircase. A tic in my jaw starts to twitch as I formulate a plan. I need to explain why I did it and calm her down. I need time or a fucking miracle. It's too late to deny any of it. I was too rash, too caught up in the moment when she confronted me. All I could see was red.

The door opens with a gentle push. I didn't bother to lock it since she's tied to the bed.

My eyes latch onto her the second I step into our bedroom. She's barely clothed, her gorgeous pale skin on full display, although most of it is flushed from her struggling and screaming.

"What do you need, sweetheart?" I ask her calmly, completely ignoring the current situation.

Her eyes narrow as she sucks in a breath, and I can feel the anger rolling off of her in waves. I nearly let out a sigh of relief. *Anger I can deal with.* The thought almost makes me smile.

"Let me out," she says although her eyes flicker down and her voice wavers with the demand.

"I can't do that if you're going to run."

"Just let me go, Mason," she pleads with a soft whimper.

She licks her lips and attempts to push herself upright. Jules winces from the binds cutting into her wrists, and I can't fucking stand it.

My hands ball into fists, but I stay put. I can't risk her trying to escape.

"You need to stay here, with me, until we figure this out," I say to her in a placating tone as I step forward, rounding the bed to get closer to her. Her breathing quickens and I'm not sure if it's due to anger or fear from me getting closer to her. My blood runs cold at the second possibility.

"We need to talk about this," I tell her gently as I sit down carefully and attempt to ease whatever worry I can. I don't want to tell her anything, and everything in me is screaming to lie and let it all be forgotten. But she's mine, and I won't do that to her. It was one thing to withhold the truth about the past, but it's another to outright lie about it.

She should know the truth, even if she doesn't like it.

"Ask me anything." My gaze is struck by hers as I speak. Her baby blues are rimmed in red, and her cheeks tearstained. She's gorgeous even like this, but not when she misbehaves. She presses her lips into a thin line, even though the bottom one trembles, and shakes her head. It seems fear is the dominant emotion. A vise tightens over my chest.

I look past her as the thick gray velvet curtain sways slightly when the heater turns on with a click. I watch it for a moment, steadying my breath and quickly come up with a solution.

"For every question," I start to say and then pause to look back at her. She's wary and when she realizes I'm offering her something, her entire body noticeably stiffens. "Every question you ask, I'll answer you honestly and untie you a bit."

It's not the best solution, seeing as how there are only four knots total keeping the rope in place. One on each wrist, and two tying her to the bed.

"You can't fight me, Jules." I harden my voice just before she can answer. "I'll let you go, but I won't let you run. Do you understand?"

She swallows and then licks her lips. "Yes," she says, the answer just above a murmur. I can tell it hurts her to speak at all, because she withdraws the moment the word slips into the tense air between us, a look of pain evident on her face.

She needs tea and to be held. She needs a gentle hand.

The bed groans as I sit, resting my hand on her bare thigh. Like a good girl she doesn't move, but she does close her eyes as if she can't stand my touch. I gently rub my thumb in soothing circles and I stare down at where our skin meets as I wait for her.

She'll forgive me, I know she will. It's only a matter of time and I'll let her lead. But only if she moves in the right direction. Closer to the two of us regaining what we had only hours ago. I just need time and given the fact my development company is now dissolved, I have plenty of it.

"Why did you do it?" she asks.

My head lifts at her question, and I meet her gaze head-on. There's nothing but sadness in those gorgeous doe eyes. "He was responsible for a woman's death."

Before I've even finished saying the words, she's already shaking her head. Already in denial. "No, I don't believe you." Her voice cracks, a telltale sign of her refusal to accept the truth as she rips her gaze from me and stares straight ahead at the door.

"I'm not lying to you, Jules." It's a struggle to keep my

voice tender, thinking back on what came over me when I decided Jace Anderson deserved to die.

"You lied," she practically hisses at me, taking me by surprise. She screams with outrage, "You're a liar!"

"I never lied to you," I answer evenly, correcting her and ignoring her outburst while I tighten my grip on the edge of the bed. I have to wait a moment for her to calm down before reaching up and slowly untying the knot on her left wrist. A deal is a deal. Even if I fucking hate her response. Her tender skin is bright pink, and it makes my chest feel tight with guilt. I never wanted to hurt her. Never. I retake my seat as she whispers, "You didn't tell the truth."

My throat dries and a rawness takes over, dampening every nerve ending along my skin. I don't have many memories of my mother, but the ones I do, the ones that are clear, are the ones where she calls my father a liar. The images flash in front of me, and my body goes cold. "I'm not a liar. I did what I had to do."

"I could never do what you did," she says.

Everyone can kill. I keep the thought to myself, hating how true it is. It's only a matter of what would push someone to do it.

"Do you have any other questions?"

"Are you going to kill me?" she asks as if it's a real possibility. Her breathing is hesitant and then hitches when she closes her eyes tight.

Waiting for those doe eyes to look back at me, desperate for an answer, the one word I give her is filled with a promise. "Never." It makes my heart hurt that she thinks it's even an option. "I told you I'd never hurt you." Of all the things today that have me on edge, that right there is the most distressing.

The thought in her head that I'm someone who would hurt her is unacceptable.

My hand rests gently against her thigh and she's quick to pull away, as if I've scorched her skin. I still at the sobering sight of her.

Her blue eyes have never looked so cold as she looks up at me and says, "No." Her next words carry so much conviction, so much hate. "Don't touch me… please."

I clench my jaw and hesitate. This is too much. Too far, and too much. I'm quick to untie all the remaining binds, blood rushing in my ears and my fingers seemingly going numb. I drop the thin rope and it pools into a puddle around her, but she doesn't move to get up. She doesn't do anything but lean farther away from me.

Her mouth opens as I push off the bed and stand to leave, but she doesn't say anything. There's only silence.

"You may hate me now, Jules, but I still love you, and you're not going anywhere until you know that and until you understand why it had to happen."

The door closes behind me with a loud click and I don't stop walking until I get to the office to retrieve the house keys. I'll lock the door. I'll keep her here until she understands.

There's no fucking way I'm letting her leave. She'll figure it out eventually; she's always been mine. It was only a matter of me finding her.

four

Julia

ALTHOUGH MY EYES ARE TIRED AND MY HEAD and limbs ache, I don't move. Not an inch. Not since I took the engagement ring off my finger and flung it across the room.

I'm far too aware of every event that led to this. It's as if I've lived my life under the warm silk sheets of the most welcoming bed, only to be kicked out, landing face-first on the cold, cracked concrete floor.

More than anything, one word keeps coming to mind. *Unprepared.* I have no idea what to do, or even what to think. It's all a mess. My life is a jumbled mess of chaos and tragedy. It's hard enough to grasp the fact that Jace was murdered. Much harder still to think that I fell in love with his murderer.

I need to get away. Far away from Mason just so I can think straight.

I can't focus on anything else other than that one truth: I need to get the hell out of this room.

The bedroom door's locked from the outside; the telltale jingle of keys and then the loud click of the lock a few moments ago alerted me to that. I already know it's the case without even trying to turn the knob. I suppose that's better than having to face him. To my left, the curtain sways and draws my eyes.

My throat closes at the thought of seeing him again. I loved him. My heart feels like a vise is clamped around it, squeezing tighter each time I think about who Mason really is and what I've done. I fell in love with my husband's killer.

The shock is still there, but it's not enough to keep the sickness of my reality at bay.

My head feels dizzy—from exhaustion maybe, I'm not sure, but I don't have time to think. I don't have time for anything until I'm far away from here.

I stare at the lone window in this room. I know it's an idiotic notion to think I can climb down from the second story and land safely below, but I have no other choice and I refuse not to try.

If there's one thing the recollection of the events leading up to this have screamed at me, it's that I need to take action and stop allowing life to railroad me.

I don't have my keys, my phone or wallet. With the groan of the bed seemingly chiding me as I stand up and make my way to the window, I peek outside to see there's already a thin layer of snow on the ground. Given its late November in New York, I'm not shocked but it's still frustrating. If I make it down there alive without breaking my neck, he'll be able to see where I've gone. A part of me huffs at the thought, knowing this is foolish, trying to escape.

But I only need to flag someone down on the road or bang on a neighbor's door. *I have to try, and I'm not waiting another second.*

The floor in the bedroom is creaky and every little sound forces me to check that the door is still closed. I know he'll be able to hear me from downstairs if he's listening. I'm careful with each step and do my best to limit the noise as I move around. I inhale deeply through clenched teeth as I open the dresser as quietly as I can but it's loud just the same as I slowly pull on the drawer. I've never noticed it before, but right now every single noise is far too loud.

My heart rampages in protest at each squeak and groan from the wooden floors. *I'm only getting dressed,* I tell myself over and over. If he comes up now, if he hears me and storms into the room to check on me, I'm only getting dressed. Surely that's what he must think.

My eyes burn with unshed tears thinking about Mason coming up here. Realizing the fear I now have for a man I once loved makes my chest feel unbearably tight.

What if he catches me?

What will he do when he's realized I've left?

Even worse: *What would he do to me?*

I swallow down the insecurity and fear; I can't be paralyzed by them. I can't wait here in this damn room for him to decide what to do with me. I'm stronger than that.

The first shirt and pair of leggings I pull out are good enough and then from the drawer below, I grab a pair of jeans to pull over top of the leggings. It's freezing outside. I don't have a coat because they're all downstairs in the hall closet, but I layer a sweater and then another one over my long-sleeved shirt. It's hard to tell if the burning heat is from the fabrics or from the anxiety that rages through me.

My fingers shake as I pull down the long cashmere sleeves. If he came up now, he'd know for sure that this is more than me just getting dressed. I'm dressed to leave. The thoughts don't slow me, they only push me to be faster; I'm fueled by nerves and the desperation to save myself.

I can barely breathe as I kneel and tie the shoelaces on a pair of sneakers I grabbed from the walk-in closet. My hands don't stop trembling and my vision keeps going in and out as the dull pain behind my eyes gets worse. I sway as my light-headedness becomes too much, and I have to close my eyes and breathe. Just breathe.

I stand on wobbly legs and walk as quietly as I can to the window, which is just as unhelpful as it was a moment ago. Staring over my shoulder at the closed door, I lick my dry, cracked lips as I unlock the window. The lock on the left turns easily but the one on the right is tight, and I need both hands and all my focus to loosen it. Each second that passes seems too long, as if this small moment is enough time for him to stop me.

Tick, tick, tick.

The sound of my heavy breathing and the blood rushing in my ears are all I hear as I push the window up as high as I can. I manage to lift the heavy thing about two feet, and I hope it'll be enough. I know there's a way to somehow angle the window and get the screen out, but in my haste and nervousness, I can't figure it out.

The heater clicks on again and I nearly have a heart attack, my scream barely contained as it tries to escape from my throat.

Tick, tick, tick.

I can't wait any longer. As the heat drifts up from the vent and mixes with the frigid November air that blows across my face, I panic.

My only thought is to rip out the screen. Without wasting another tick of the internal clock, I snatch a shirt from the hamper to my right and wrap it around my hand. My footsteps were far too loud, but time is more important.

I take one more look back at the door before punching through the screen. It breaks surprisingly easily and I nearly fall forward, the torn mesh scraping against my forearm. I contain my gasp and ignore how my heart seems to leap up my throat as I look down two stories to the cold hard ground below. It's a sobering sight.

There's a thin layer of white snow coating the grass and although the weather has let up, the air is sharp from the biting wind. I take a deep breath, pulling the ripped screen back and tearing it open more, protecting my hand with the clothing. Somehow ripping it wider is more difficult than making the initial tear.

My breathing comes in faster, and the light-headed sensation returns when the hole is large enough for me to climb through.

All the spiked edges of the broken screen are going to catch on my sweater, I already know. Once I get footing out on the sill, I'll have to try to grip onto the pillar to my right and slowly climb down while balancing myself on the stones that line the house. It's practically impossible. My head shakes of its own accord at the thought, refusing to feel defeated. I have to do this. I have no other choice.

The threads of my sweater snag like I knew they would the moment I climb through the window and brush against the screen, but I press forward. As my left foot finds purchase on the windowsill, the wind blows so forcefully that I cling to the frame with my right hand and consider abandoning the idea completely. *I've gone absolutely mad.* My nose and cheeks burn from the biting cold, and I have to close my eyes.

Breathe. Just breathe.

I refuse to go back in there. The second the wind stops, I finish crawling out and balance on the ledge, my knuckles bright white from holding on so tightly. Each time I have to readjust my grip, I'm filled with a renewed sense of terror. Only the balls of my feet are balanced on the thin ledge, and my hands already ache from clutching the window in the bitter cold.

I make the mistake of looking down and seeing how far I'd drop and how there's nothing to break my fall if the wind were to blow too hard. Or if my grip gives out, or if something else happens and I fail. *I don't want to die.*

A few moments pass and I simply can't move. The wind whips my hair around my face and I shut my eyes tight, frozen by the vision of me plummeting to my death.

This is taking too much time. I need to get going. My left foot moves first, all the way to the edge of the sill and as far as I can get with both of my hands still gripping the window frame.

I have to let go in order to lean over, and I do it so

quickly and with so much force that I nearly push myself off. My head spins from the height, but I keep moving. My right hand grips the window and my left reaches for the brick closest to the pillar. My nails scratch at the rough stone, but my grip is solid.

I feel stuck for the longest time. The cold makes my hands numb and the wind is coming and going so frequently that I'm afraid the second I move, it will violently rip me away from the pillar, but I manage the motion in a single leap.

A scream is torn from my throat as I fall an inch or two until my sneaker hits the decorative carving on the pillar and I'm able to wrap my arms around it. Adrenaline roars inside of me and I pray Mason didn't hear. And then I make another silent prayer: that this foolish plan will work.

Slowly, ever so slowly, I climb down inch by inch. The only places I dare to look are directly in front of me and up to the open window. I watch the curtains sway inside of the bedroom as I slip down the pillar at a snail's pace, relying on the tread of my sneakers against the carved marble pillar for purchase.

I don't even realize I've made it safely until I try to slide farther down and can't. There's ground beneath my feet.

Astonished and still very much consumed by fear, I note my sweater is torn with pulls everywhere, and I'm so cold I can hardly move my limbs. I look up once more at the open window and realize it's only a matter of time before he realizes I'm gone.

Run. I don't hesitate one more second. My sore limbs come to life as I take off down Mason's driveway and I don't look back.

I NEED TO MAKE TWO THINGS CLEAR TO HER.

1. I love her, and I always will.
2. She's not leaving me.

We're going to work through this one way or another. Even if I have to drug her. I know the chances of a roofie working at this point are slim to none, but depending on her reaction, it's the only thing I can think of and the only easy out to make things right again. If only she would forget.

As I draw closer to the top of the stairs, a cold draft wraps itself around me. At first, I'm confused, then furious. She didn't. She wouldn't… my denial is pointless. I already know she did.

My pace picks up and I bang on the bedroom door. My knuckles slam against the hard wood door and I yell out, "Jules!"

How long has it been, maybe a half hour at most since I locked her in there? My heart hammers in my chest. She's gone. *She's left me.*

It's no use. I can already feel the cold air seeping into the hall from under the door. The keys are already in my hand as I pound my fist against the door again like a fucking fool, nearly breaking down the door. They rattle as I find the right one and shove it into the lock before throwing open the door. I'm greeted with an empty bed and the biting cold blowing in through a torn window screen.

I stare at the window for only a second before taking long strides across the room, pulling the curtain back to look down at the ground outside. I half expect to see her lying dead on the grass.

She'd rather risk this than deal with me.

My throat closes at the bitter thought, and the harsh wind whispers, taunting me that she simply jumped to end it all. Relief is unexpected but welcome when I peer out and trace the footsteps in the snow. She hasn't been gone long judging by how clean and clear the prints are.

My lungs threaten to fail me as I take off out the room and down the stairs, and I don't stop moving as I snatch my car keys and phone off the front hall table. She's out there with a head start and I only have so much time to catch her. My coat's in the living room, but I don't bother with it. I don't bother with anything other than climbing into my Mercedes and reversing out of the driveway as quickly as I can.

A thin layer of sweat covers my skin and only adds to the freezing effect of the air.

If she tells anyone… I'm fucked.

"She can't," I say under my breath and curse, the vision of her testifying against me flashing in front of my eyes. There's hardly any snow on the asphalt, and her footprints disappear in less than a quarter mile. With my hands gripping and twisting the leather steering wheel, I continue to drive ahead. I glance down every small gap I pass, although the main road is vacant. It's early morning and I know there are plenty of cars that drive by here on their way to work. She could have flagged someone down.

She's gone. My throat tightens with the realization and I pound my fist against the window.

She doesn't have any evidence. My thoughts take over. She has no proof, and there's nothing the police would ever find. She couldn't possibly go to them. There's no fucking way. But if not to the police, then where?

My heart's racing as I pull over, and I don't know what the hell she's thinking.

That you're a murderer. That you'll hurt her.

I ignore the damning truth and keep pushing down the ache that takes over.

It doesn't take long before I decide my next move should be to search her home. If not there, then I need to find her friend's addresses. My tires squeal as I pull back onto the road, intent on finding her and bringing her back here. I don't need anyone else trying to keep her away from me.

I lean over and click the radio off, only just now realizing it's on and then turn the heat all the way up. I'm numb from the combination of the wintry air and the thoughts that won't quit yelling in my head that I'm fucked. Turning on my blinker to head onto a busier street, I struggle to take in an easy breath.

Act normal. Come up with a plan.

There was a nasty rumor going around that Jules has had issues with alcohol ever since Jace's death. I'd never talk about her as if she were a drunk, but I have to use something that would make people question why she'd accuse me of murder.

I tap my thumb against the steering wheel.

I don't know if it would work. It'd be her word against mine. And there's no real evidence.

But if I went down that route, I'd definitely lose her and everyone in this city would question if there was any truth to what she claimed.

My family name would be called into question.

My business reputation would be ruined.

More than that, the only person I ever loved would be my downfall.

A bitter huff of a humorless laugh leaves me as I look to my left and turn down the street.

I could go away for life if the police do believe her and look into it. If they find something, or if the person who sent that note comes forward with their proof. I don't give a fuck about that, though. I haven't known what love is since my mother died. But I know it's what I feel for Jules.

I've given her the power to ruin me. That's what true love is.

If I let her get away, she'll do it.

She'll destroy every piece of me.

As I struggle to come to terms with the realization, my phone rings from the passenger seat where I'd thrown it earlier. I lean over and pick it up, answering without looking to see who it is while I drive down Jules's street.

"Hello," I answer, hoping it's her. Hoping she's only asking for time or space. I won't give her either, but at least then I'll know we have a chance.

"Mason," my father says.

"Father," I say, feeling disappointment that it's not her, followed by distrust. We haven't spoken since I knocked him out in his office. What the hell does he want?

His voice is full of confidence but more than that, imperiousness. "I have a little something I think you want." I pull up alongside Jules's street but the only parking space available is a few doors down from her place, and I slow down to lean forward and look out the windshield. It's starting to get light outside, but not so much that I wouldn't see lights on inside her house. I scan the windows as I absently say, "And what would that be?"

"I got a call from Commissioner Haynes." My body stills as my father continues.

His words snap my attention to him. *Commissioner.* "It seems your recent love interest has something urgent to confess."

If my father thinks she's a threat, that's a much more concerning issue.

"She doesn't know anything." I'm quick to respond. I speed down the street, cutting someone off and they lean on their horn. I have to weave through the few cars out this early in the morning to get down to Fourth Street. I need to get to her. "Don't touch her," I say.

"I wouldn't dare," my father says, and I can practically see the smug smile on his face. *Jules.* I grit my teeth in anger.

"I imagine you'll be here soon?" he asks with a thin veil of arrogance.

"I'm ten minutes from the station," I answer grudgingly. I hate that he's involved and interfering, but if he wasn't, she would have talked. She has no idea what she's done. She's put herself in danger.

My foot presses down harder on the gas pedal with each passing thought. I need to get to Jules before she says a fucking word.

CHAPTER

six

Julia

I'VE BEEN PICKING AT THE SAME SNARLED THREAD ON my sweater for nearly fifteen minutes now.

My sneaker taps nervously against the leg of the simple wooden table; they're still damp from the snow. Something feels off and wrong. Crossing my arms, I look away from the mirror. Anywhere but the mirror.

The stranger in the car kept asking me over and over what was wrong, but I could barely speak. I was so cold, and nothing would come out except that I needed the police. I was lucky he pulled over and offered me a ride. The concern in his pale blue eyes was comforting but only so much that it allowed me to get in the car. His checkered sweater slid down his bony arms as he drove, and he kept looking over at me in the passenger seat. He had to be in his fifties, or maybe sixties. The wrinkles around his eyes told me he was at least my father's age.

That comfort is long gone and a different sensation took over the second he stopped in front of the station. I have no proof, no evidence. I don't know if anyone is going to believe me. I need to tell someone, though. I swallow thickly, realizing I don't know where to begin or if a soul will believe me or do anything at all.

The old man stayed with me while a young officer gave me a blanket and told me it was all right. *Whatever it is, you're safe now.* Dressed in his blues, the man was maybe in his mid-twenties and didn't have a clue what I was there for. It was such a spectacle, but even though they were kind and open I still couldn't spit out the words.

Then I was handed over to Detective Myer.

He's much too young for someone in his position, clean-shaven and tall with dark brown eyes. He has to be around the same age as the officer who greeted me warmly. There's no warmth to Myer, though; he's all corded muscle, although he doesn't have the broad shoulders or height to him to balance out his body. Even with his badge and prying stare, he doesn't have an air around him that commands authority.

There's something else as well, something about the way he looks at me that makes me feel as though I'm not safe. Like I should have changed my mind and headed back out into the snow and never stopped running. I don't trust the detective. I didn't when he told me to sit in here and twenty minutes later, what little hope and faith I had has faded.

Maybe I'm being paranoid and it's all in my head, but it

seems wrong he never asked any questions. He simply told me to follow him back here and sat me down while he went to talk to the commissioner. I'm alone and left wondering what the hell I'm doing here at all.

Guilt worms its way through every bone in my body. Every tick of the clock tempts me to get up from this table. I'm going to choke on my words. I can't do this. They'll never believe me and I can't say the truth out loud.

Just as the notion hits me, the door opens and I stand mostly out of instinct, but also possibly fear. The need to run is overwhelming, but when my eyes catch sight of the imposing man walking in behind Detective Myer and another man who I assume is the commissioner, my knees go weak.

I don't need to be told he's Mason's father. I don't need to be introduced. His gray eyes and sharp cheekbones give it away. He even clears his throat like Mason as he unbuttons his suit jacket and sits in the empty chair across from me.

My eyes flicker to Detective Myer's, who simply crosses his arms and leans against the wall in the far left corner. His dark eyes bore into me and send a chill down my spine. The commissioner makes a show of closing the door and then taking a seat at the far end of the table.

"Sit, sit," Mason's father insists. "Jules, isn't it?" he says with a smile that doesn't reach his eyes.

My knees are so weak that I obey him, falling into my seat and staring at the commissioner who isn't looking at me at all. He casually picks at his nails instead. I glance back to the mirror and pray there's a camera recording or someone behind it watching this. Someone else. God, please help me.

I'm not safe here. That's the only thing I'm sure of. *What have I gotten myself into?*

"Good girl," Mason's father says approvingly, and it sickens me to my core. There's something about the air of ownership he projects. Something about the way his words roll off his tongue. The fear is only partially brushed aside by my disgust, but I'm at least able to look him in the eye.

"Where's Mason?" I ask evenly, although I don't know how I got the courage to speak.

His father's eyes twinkle with something that brightens the gray. Something that makes my stomach churn.

"Don't worry, he's coming shortly." Mr. Thatcher looks over his shoulder at the detective. As his mouth parts to say something his straight white teeth peek out from behind his thin lips, but he's interrupted by the door banging open.

"I'm sorry, Detective Myer," a young woman says from the hallway as Mason stands in the doorway, hovering in the opening with an authority that's incomparable.

And he's pissed.

The way his steel gray eyes seem to turn a sharp silver and pierce through me makes every tiny hair on my body stand on end. Every inch of my skin chills and then heats so quickly I can't move. All I can do is stare into his eyes, caught in his gaze.

He breaks it before I can relax, and only then can I breathe.

My eyes drop to the floor as the shock withdraws, and my reality strikes me across the face. The emotions that swarm me are confusing to say the least. I'm relieved to see the very man I fled from only hours ago.

"Jules," he says and Mason's voice isn't cold like I imagined it would be. I lift my eyes to his, and my heart beats in rhythm with the seconds that tick by ever so slowly. *Tick,*

tick, tick. The room is silent as the other men wait for my reaction. I can't give them anything, though. I'm numb and useless with exhaustion and a thread of fear so easily broken. My throat is dry, and I can barely manage to make eye contact with Mason. I pick at my sleeve and look back at the table, feeling defeated, foolish and guilty.

How is it possible that guilt is what consumes me most?

"Sweetheart, what are you doing here?" Mason asks me with sympathy in his voice as he pulls out the chair next to me. The legs scrape on the floor and Mason wraps his arm around the back of my chair as he sits close to me, but not an inch of him touches me. Not his arm, not his knee to mine. He's so close I can feel the heat of his body, but he's distant all the same.

"Is something wrong?" he asks me, and I immediately shake my head no.

I'm retreating like a coward. "I want to go home," I say, whispering the plea just above a murmur, still not looking any of the men in the eye.

"What's that?" Detective Myer says from the corner of the room, pushing off the wall and uncrossing his arms for the first time since he's been in here. He starts to walk over.

I clear my throat and ignore how scratchy my voice is as I repeat myself. "I want to go home."

The detective leans against the table, his palms flat as he waits for me to look up at him. His voice is strong and hard, filled with contempt as he says, "Issuing a false report and taking up the time—"

"What false report?" Mason asks at the same time that I refute the detective.

"No one has taken a statement from me. I haven't said

anything," I say and my voice is stronger than I imagined it would be.

Mason rises from his chair abruptly, leaning over the table and bracing his forearms in front of me as he gets in Myer's face. "Don't you dare," Mason says, speaking with a tone of malice that makes me flinch. "Don't you dare threaten her."

Mason's chiseled jaw is covered with stubble and the way it clenches while his hands fist on the table takes the commissioner by surprise. He visibly balks, and it's then that Mason's father pipes up.

"Now, now. Miss Summers had something she wanted to say, Mason." Mason's head tilts slowly, daring his father to speak again and the old man does just that, the glint in his eye ever present.

He looks past Mason and asks me, "What was it that brought you here, Julia?"

"Nothing," I say and my voice croaks.

"Oh, come now," he says. Mr. Thatcher's voice is lighthearted, but it's never been more apparent how dark the situation has become. Do they already know? *They must.*

And now they know that I know.

My throat tightens instantly, as if a strong hand has gripped it to choke me. "You can come to me with anything, Miss Summers," Mason's father says, staring me straight in the eyes as he continues, "I know everyone, Jules, and I'll be sure you're taken care of—"

"Enough," Mason practically growls at his father.

His father finally takes his assessing stare from me to give Mason his attention. "Just out of curiosity, Mason, what little secret did you tell our Jules?"

Mason ignores his father, taking my hand in his with a bruising force and leading me to the door. My legs are weak but I keep up with him. He rips the door open so violently I swear he nearly pulls it off the hinges.

"Go," Mason commands me, sweeping his arm forward and I listen immediately, grateful to be getting the fuck out of here mostly unscathed.

"Bye for now, Jules," Mr. Thatcher says to my back as I leave, and I'm grateful Mason is between us. I can't breathe or do anything other than follow Mason's lead until we've left the station. I can feel everyone watching us and my face blazes with the awareness, but fear is what keeps me moving and my eyes staring straight ahead.

"Mason," I whimper as he braces his hand against the small of my back and leads me across the street to where he's parked. I stare at his car, feeling as though I'm so close to safety, but knowing I'm going back to a cell.

Mason doesn't respond but he pulls me in close, wrapping his arm around my waist as we cross the street to the parking lot. Without knowing what to think or feel, my head spins. I have to walk quickly to keep up with his purposeful strides, but I feel comforted just from his arm wrapped around me, needing his embrace.

For a moment, as Mason opens my door and waits for me to get in his car, I think there's hope. I think I can repair the damage I've caused even though I'm not sure why I'm even considering it.

I'm so confused, so conflicted. The only thing I'm certain of is that if Mason hadn't come to get me, something bad would have happened. Something to make sure I was silenced.

Foolish. I'm so damn foolish. At the thought, I struggle to breathe and I lay my head back against the seat, feeling the weight of what just happened flow through every limb. Heat flows around my skin, uncomfortably and unbearably so.

Mason shuts his door with a loud thud as he gets in and starts the car, all without sparing me a glance while he backs out and merges into traffic.

With tension pulled through every inch of me, I wait for something, for a moment to speak or for him to say something, but I'm given nothing.

"Mason?" I take a chance and say his name as the car stops at a red light. His fingers flex on the steering wheel and then his knuckles turn white as he grips it and slowly turns to look at me.

His eyes are cold, ice cold, and I instantly regret speaking at all.

"We'll talk when we get home," he says beneath his breath. I nod once, feeling alone and abandoned and utterly hopeless.

Forever doesn't end,
But it also doesn't last.
What you feel right now,
Will soon be the past.

Left only with the memories,
And the desire to hold,
But time doesn't wait,
And even love grows old.

I WOULD HAVE KILLED THEM. BOTH THE DETECTIVE and the commissioner. Possibly even my father. I've never been so close to snapping, never. I've never come close to feeling that pull. Pure anger and hatred are fueling my thoughts. I'm barely contained, on the edge of something dangerous, something so dark I've never confronted it before. Not even that fateful day I destroyed Jules's life. Even that wasn't like this.

Dragging my hand down my face, I listen as my shoes smack against the hardwood floors, but then the sound is muted on the rug in front of the gray suede sofa in my living room.

"What were you going to tell them?" I ask as I pace in front of her, my gaze still focused downward.

It's never felt colder or darker in this house before. Not to me. Even with the bright white snow reflecting light through the large modern windows on the back wall, there's not an ounce of warmth in the room.

Ice courses through my blood, but even that's not cold enough to take the heat from my anger.

I can't stop moving; every muscle is coiled and ready to fight. She doesn't know what she does to me. She has no fucking idea what she's done. What kind of danger she's put herself in.

"How could you?" I say. The question is menacing and it stops me in my tracks. It holds a vicious tone I can't contain. I take a single glance up and regret it. With her beautiful blue eyes widened, Jules looks as though I've slapped her, flinching and her mouth dropping open, but she doesn't answer.

"I—" she tries to speak, but can't finish her sentence. It's fucking infuriating. I don't know what's worse, how she's impulsively made everything worse for us, or the fact that she left to turn me in. My jaw clenches so hard I nearly crack my teeth. I have to stare past her at the blanket of snow as she squirms on the sofa. "Mason, I—"

"You what?" My voice booms from my chest as my heart pounds. She would be dead if my father hadn't called me. He could have killed her. Or have had her killed rather, so he wouldn't have blood on his own hands. He'd have done it too, if he hadn't wanted to toy with me. If he hadn't wanted something to hold over my head. If he hadn't wanted me to know that I owe him now. "You have no idea what you've done."

I can only imagine my father is under the impression that she knows about his involvement with Avery's death. That I told her. That she was there to rat *him* out and not me.

"Fuck." The curse lays under my breath as my pacing continues. It takes every ounce of self-control not to destroy this place.

He doesn't know a damn thing about Jace's murder. No one does but the anonymous stranger who sent Jules that note.

My father won't let Jules live. I take in a ragged breath, but it doesn't calm me.

There's no fucking way I'll let him touch her. She's mine, and she'll be my wife and mother to my children. If he dares try any of that shit with her again, I'll destroy him. I'll end his life so fucking miserably that he'll be thankful when I finally slide the edge of a knife across his throat.

"Mason," she says and fear clings to the single whispered word.

"They would have killed you, Jules." I swallow the ball of spikes in my throat and finally look down at her glassed-over eyes. Her baby blues are full of so much emotion. "They would have killed you," I repeat in a whisper and it's that sickening thought that breaks the rage. It shatters into something else. Something that feels like weakness.

Jules holds my gaze, but she doesn't answer me. Tears leak from the corner of her eyes, but Jules doesn't acknowledge them. Her face displays an expression of sincerity. "I'm scared," she says. She gently shakes her head and looks past me, down the hallway and avoiding eye contact. My heart clenches in my chest.

"I didn't want any of this," she says and her voice is raw with emotion.

I swallow thickly and tell her the simple truth, "You never should have left."

She looks up at me with daggers in her eyes as she hisses at me without a second passing between us, "You never should have killed my husband."

It catches me off guard for a moment, but the pure venom and hate she had only hours ago is dimmed, the stark reality of the situation taking its toll on her. I keep my eyes on hers as I tell her, "Your husband deserved to die for what he did."

Jules's lips part as she takes in a heavy breath, looking as if she's going to respond, but no words come out. After a moment she looks away, finally wiping the tears from her reddened cheeks with the sleeve of her ruined sweater and sniffling.

"I don't want to die, Mason," she says weakly. Her chest rises and falls with her steady breathing. "I just want to go home and I'll never say a word."

"You can't go home." My voice is hard and leaves no room for negotiation. I won't risk putting her in danger. I don't know what my father's told the commissioner. I need to make it clear to him that she knows nothing about what happened. I'll lie. I'll tell him I hit her.

He's always seen through my lies, though. He's a damn good liar, and the challenge of outsmarting him has never seemed so daunting.

I could tell him the truth. I'll tell him anything I need to in order to make him believe she's not a threat.

"If you leave me, you're putting yourself at risk—" I can't finish because it's at that moment that Jules finally breaks down. Her always composed demeanor cracks and her shoulders hunch forward as a sob wracks her body.

Any explanation dies at the back of my throat. All of my anger dissipates. She's broken because of me. This happened because of me. I fucking hate myself.

"I'll protect you," I tell her. I only hesitate for a moment before taking the seat next to her. My weight causes her small body to lean into mine, and I'm surprised when she doesn't resist. She lets me hold her for a moment as her cries get softer and she wipes the tears from beneath her eyes. I've craved this warmth since she found out the truth. "I promise."

I lean forward and kiss her hair, taking in her sweet scent but it makes her withdraw. She doesn't look at me, and the moment she has her composure back she pulls away from me.

"Is it really that bad to stay with me?"

Her body stiffens at the question, and she doesn't answer.

"You have no other options but to stay where I tell you and do what I say. You need to convince everyone in this city that you're mine, that everything between us is better than it's ever been."

"I just want to go home." She'll never know how much that desire damages me in the worst way. How empty and hollow her confession leaves me. "I won't tell anyone," she adds, peeking up through her thick lashes.

"You don't have a choice," I tell her as I cup her cheek in my hand. I run the rough pad of my thumb along her lush lips, and they beg me to kiss her. Her pale skin is flushed a beautiful shade of pink and everything in me wants to hold her close. I want to take her pain away; I want to remind her who she belongs to.

"You're mine, Jules. There's no changing that."

CHAPTER
eight

Julia

> *Pressed against a hard wall,*
> *No choices, no way out.*
> *Without the air to breathe,*
> *And only left with doubt.*
>
> *There's no way to move forward,*
> *No will to make amends.*
> *Nothing but what he gives me,*
> *Trapped and at dead ends.*

I'M DESPERATE FOR MY MOTHER, OF ALL THINGS. Desperate to call her, to confess what's happened, to plead with her to protect me. As if something so simple could save me.

I pick at the comforter on the bed and wish I had my computer or my phone. Or any way at all to contact someone.

Not a single soul has come up Mason's driveway since he brought me back here. There are no neighbors close enough to just drop by, not that Mason's the neighborly type. Even the mailbox is all the way at the end of the long driveway. I'm trapped in this house that's practically a gilded cage without a damn thing to do other than write down every forsaken emotion and thought that comes to me. Time is moving slowly; the past three days have felt like a year, and all I can do is be consumed by the thoughts of how I got here. *How did this become my life?*

The moment I look out a window or walk toward a door, Mason's there. Watching me, waiting to see what I'll do. He went from being my lover and my hope, to a prison warden. Every time he enters the room, I can *feel* him.

Yet he's pretending he's not monitoring me, that he trusts I'll behave because I'm afraid. Part of that's true, but mostly I'm waiting, simply biding my time. I'll be quiet and listen until I have a chance to leave him. He can't keep me here forever.

The bathroom door opens with a soft creak, stealing me away from my thoughts as Mason steps into the bedroom from the en suite. He's bare-chested, his tanned skin on display as he strides toward the dresser with only a towel wrapped around his waist. His demeanor is casual, as if nothing happened. As if I can live with the fact that he's a murderer, and my life is in danger because of him and his father. If I'd known he was tied to anything at all like this, I'd never have gone home with him that first night. I'd never have flirted, I'd never have touched him, let alone fallen in love with him.

I have to bite my cheek to keep from screaming, to keep from doing something stupid as Mason turns his back to me, letting the towel drop as he selects a pair of boxers from the top drawer of his dresser. Between the multiple heartaches and chaos, loss is there. Loss of someone I thought I loved who didn't exist. Loss of the independence I was so sure I had.

"I bought you a dress for Saturday," he informs me matter-of-factly as he unzips a garment bag with his back to me.

My eyes flicker to the beautiful evening gown hanging on the back of the closet door. Its jewels sparkle as the light hits it; they're sparser on top, just a faint pattern that forms the outline of an hourglass, overlaying the darker gray on the sides and absent on the light gray inlay. From the hips down, the gown is completely covered in the dazzling Swarovski crystals.

It's stunning. I'm sure it would impress everyone at the charity event. I don't remember which one this is; I only know that Mason wants to attend to discuss business with a number of investors and it's an annual charity gala I've gone to without fail for years.

For a moment, I can only watch Mason continue with the business of getting dressed, wondering how he could even consider the two of us attending an event together. "I don't see how I could possibly go." I can't imagine standing in a room smiling and playing nice when I feel like this. When

I'm trapped and cornered. When I'm literally scared for my life.

Mason's steel gray eyes pierce through me as if he heard every one of my thoughts when I look at his reflection in the cheval mirror.

"You've had a couple of nights to think about things. You'll have another handful of days to come around," he says confidently and breaks my gaze to shut a drawer, holding a pair of socks in his right hand.

"Where are you going?" I ask him, feeling a touch of hope rise in my chest at the prospect of him leaving. *I just want to go home.* The thought plays in my head on a loop like a broken record.

His lips press into a thin line and he turns slowly to face me, leaning back against the dresser. "Do you think it would be wise?" he asks. He hasn't moved but somehow he seems much closer than he was a moment ago.

I feel the blood drain from my face. "What do you mean?"

"Jules, my sweetheart," he says as he sets the clothes on top of the dresser and strides toward me. The bed dips as he sits on the edge, my heart racing from the proximity even though he doesn't touch me. "I'm still the man I was," he says calmly; his voice is soft and it breaks something inside of me. The smile he gives me is sad and doesn't reach his eyes. Leaning forward, he adds, "I can practically hear what you're thinking."

Thud, my heart pauses, caught in a trap that snaps shut around it. I swallow and focus on calming down to pry it free from the steel bars, attempting to pretend I don't know what he's talking about.

My head shakes to deny the truth but he reaches out, grabbing me by the nape of the neck and my hip, holding me in place and forcing me to look at him. It's possessive, it's dominating and it steals my breath. He hasn't been this close to me in days. His lips are so very close to mine. Just like my heart, I'm trapped.

"I'm not going to lose you, Jules." He speaks with an intensity that makes the world blur around him.

"I'm not leaving," I whisper with a shaky breath, although even I can tell it's a lie. My words are just as weak as I am when it comes to him. The corner of his lips twitch as if he wants to smile and pretend I'm telling the truth, but he doesn't.

"I'm the same man you fell in love with." The steel gray gaze softens, begging me to understand and believe him, but I can't. The tension is thick between us, but how can he expect me to simply forget? When I look at him, I see it all play out, over and over again.

I refuse to believe I ever knew this man, but the very thought splits my heart down the center.

I could never love a murderer. I could never be with the person who killed Jace. Pain lances through my chest, and I have to look away. As much as I wish I could turn it off and stop loving him entirely, I know that's not a possibility either. A piece of my heart is his forever, but that only makes me hate him more.

A question begs to be asked. One I've thought every night since he confessed. "You knew when you saw me that first night?" I ask him with a raw voice. That's what I simply can't wrap my head around. He knew who I was. He knew how much he'd hurt me and ruined me. Yet it didn't stop him.

"Knew what?" he asks, sitting easily across from me and

I look him in the eyes to confront him as I say, "You knew who I was? Jace's widow."

He nods once.

"How could you?" I ask as my blood races and whatever took over a moment ago vanishes. It's yet again another betrayal. "Was I a prize to you? A reward for getting away with it?" I say out of spite.

His expression changes to one I'm growing familiar with. To distaste and anger. Apparently we both feel it. "Don't you dare." His nostrils flare as he adds, "Don't you dare do that to us. To what we have."

"Had," I say and my throat hurts as the word leaves my lips. I don't see how I could ever forgive him or how he can expect that I would. He may be the only thing keeping me alive and standing in the way of his father silencing me, but he'll forever be my husband's murderer. A liar, a sinner, and ultimately someone who used me.

"You were only Jules to me. Only a woman who was hurt and broken." His words hang in the air between us and my conviction sways. Mason hesitates then adds, "I knew your pain was because of what I'd done. I knew it was my fault, and I wanted to make it better."

My lips part with disbelief. "Make it better?"

"I don't know what to say, Jules." He lets his hands fall to the bed beside me, his fingers resting against my thigh. "I don't know what to tell you."

"There's nothing to say." I'm certain of that at least. I stare at the comforter and avoid the hurt look in his eyes. He has no right to be saddened or angered. He has no right to expect anything from me. He's the one who put all of this into motion. He could have stopped it.

"There is more to say. And in time you'll want to know more."

My shoulders rise with a heavy breath. I know it's true. I need to know if my husband did have a woman murdered. How could he? Mason must be wrong.

I just can't imagine it. I can't believe I was married to a man who would have someone killed. He was living with me, sharing my bed and kissing me every morning. I can't see it. What's worse, I don't want to see it. Just like I didn't want to see the other lies that came out after he died. *I didn't know the man I once loved.* I look up into Mason's gray eyes and I don't know which man that thought was for. Jace or Mason.

I suppose both.

"I just want to go home," I tell Mason one last time. One last plea.

"No, you're staying here. Don't try to run, Jules," he tells me and his voice is so low. He leans forward, resting his forehead against mine. "I would kill for you. I'd die for you. I love you."

His words send a chill through me, not because of the intensity, but because I feel with everything in me that each word is utterly and completely true.

nine

Mason

I can't fucking stand this. Every time she passes me, every time I look at her there's a look in her eyes that warns me to stay away. To not touch her, to not approach her, to not say a damn word to her.

I'm the same man I was when I slipped that ring around her finger. The one that lays in the drawer of my nightstand now. The one I picked up off the floor when she left me. I figured it'd be better to hide it from her than give it back and risk her flushing it.

With the ring between two of my fingers, I twist it back and forth, the cushion-cut diamond moving from side to side with moonlight glinting off it as it pours in through the gap in the curtains. I turn my gaze to the window, knowing just beyond the thick velvet fabric is a ripped screen that still needs to be replaced.

This bedroom has become a cage. A prison of her own making. I've given her time. I've been gentle, given her space, but it's only pissing me off when she glares at me. She's a stubborn woman and I understand her needs, but it feels like I'm slowly snapping, not bending.

It's time for a change. I don't know how long it takes to mourn or forgive, but I also don't give a fuck. There's too much on my mind for me to be worried about where we are with each other. I need her. More importantly, I need to know she won't run so I can keep her safe.

I can't have anyone else questioning it either. They need to be very aware that we're still in love. Every. Single. Person.

With a particular person in mind, I glance at the phone on my nightstand. My father isn't answering my calls.

I'm tempted to go to his office to make sure he backs off, but that means either leaving Jules alone or taking her with me. Between those two options of course I'd be bringing her along, but I don't want him anywhere near her. Just walking into the station, knowing he was with her, toying with her, and hearing him threaten her was almost too much for me. I take in a heavy breath, staring at the diamond to calm myself again.

He has one more chance. One meeting on Saturday to treat her the way she deserves and apologize for what happened at the station. She's everything to me, and I won't let him frighten her. It's bad enough as it is. Otherwise... I'll have no choice but to kill him. My plan at this charity, the only plan I have, is to make that promise very clear to my father.

We're in the eye of the storm, I know it. Chaos is lurking in the shadows surrounding us, and I need my sweetheart by my side. I need her clinging to me and letting me protect her.

Right now, with her on the other side of the bed, she's hardly speaking to me let alone capable of trusting me. I can't sleep at night until she does, because I don't trust her either, and it's a battle of wills. Neither of us sleeping, neither of us giving an inch. And that's exactly what will happen tonight if I don't do something.

The diamond sparkles brilliantly, the light shining from one facet to the other.

This belongs on her fucking finger.

I stand abruptly, wanting nothing more than to tell her it's never parting from her again. But the moment I see her, she's running her fingers along her wrists. At the faint bruises and small cuts left from when I tied her up days ago.

My anger leaves slowly, like a leak, leaving me empty and hollow with regret.

"I can't take it back." I clear my throat and give her the words as they come to me. "You need to stop this, Jules. We can't continue like this."

Her posture changes, the bed creaking along with the slow movements as she grips the comforter and pulls it closer to her. Her expression shifts, and she's not pretending anymore. She's not hiding her anger; she glares at me, leaning forward. It thrills me. *Give me that anger, sweetheart. Fight me, slam your fists into my chest, take it out on me. I'll show you I can take it. I can let you get it all out and then soothe it away and fuck you so hard and so thoroughly you won't remember a damn thing except for how much you love my cock inside of you.*

"Did you like it?" I ask her as my dick twitches with the need to push her and make her angrier.

A moment passes and she simply stares at me, refusing to answer.

"Did you like it when I tied you up?" I ask and this time, she can't ignore my question.

"Fuck you," she says, jumping off the bed and making her way toward the door to leave me again. She's not fucking leaving me, though. I'm quicker than her and she knows it. I slam the door shut before she can walk through. With both my palms above her pressed firmly against the door, I cage her in with my arms as she spins to face me with a gasp of shock. My arms are long and her body's small, so there's still nearly a foot of space between us, but it feels as if we're closer than we've been in so long.

Because it's real. This tension and this moment are more real than the lifeless days we've spent together living like ghosts of ourselves since I told her she wasn't leaving.

She slowly takes an inch forward, waiting for me to stop her from leaving, but I don't. By this point, she should know I'm not going to hurt her. I meant what I said. I will never hurt her.

"Just forget it all, Jules." She tries to walk around me and under my arm, ignoring me and I can't stand it. My forearms press against the door and close the space between us, trapping her there and forcing her to talk to me.

"What do you want from me?" she screams out, her lips close to mine and her anger tangible.

"Forgiveness," I answer lowly, but with a rawness I pray she can feel.

"I can't forgive you."

"I had to do it."

Her brow pinches and she looks like she's going to argue, but she stays silent, biting her tongue and attempting to go back to the version of her I've dealt with for days. She stares at anything except me, as if ignoring me will free her from this moment.

I'm not going to let her get off that easy. She has to say something; I need to force her to confront me, because I know she won't say something on her own. "You have to get over it."

"Never," she says, finally looking back at me and staring me in the eyes. "You're a monster."

"Is that what you want?" I ask her as I take a half step forward to force her back against the door, both of my hands pinning her hips in place. "For me to turn into some kind of monster so you can justify hating me?" My grip's not so strong that it hurts her, but it's forceful enough to get her attention. Her head comes forward and I crash my lips against hers, stealing a quick kiss before she can move away. I move my lips to her ear, pinning her whole body against the wall as my right hand travels up her side while my left grips the hair at the nape of her neck. She's trapped.

"There's a difference between what you've been thinking I'd do and what I've really been doing, sweetheart." I speak just above a murmur. My breathing picks up along with hers, and her nails dig into the shirt on my chest. She's not pushing me away; she's holding me right where I am. I'm just as close to her as I wanted to be.

"You think I'm a bad man in that pretty little head of yours, but you fell in love with me. With the real me and there's no hiding from that." I run the tip of my nose from her cheek to her temple, breathing in her scent. Her small body is so hot against mine. Her rapid pants only aid in making me hard as fuck for her.

"I'll never stop loving you." I speak so low, I'm not sure she hears. I open my eyes and stare at the wall, realizing how fucked up this is, aching over it, but unable to let her go. I'm too afraid of losing her forever. I won't let it happen.

"Just do it, Mason." Jules nearly chokes on her words, and I have to look down into her eyes to see the defiance there. She's pushing me. She knows I'll never hurt her. It's so fucking obvious, and the realization makes me smile slightly.

"Do what?" I ask.

"Whatever you want with me," she says, although her gaze drops to my chest with nothing but defeat in her eyes. "Or let your father kill me."

"Is that what you want?"

"You won't let me leave," is the only answer she gives me.

"That doesn't answer my question." My heart pounds in protest at the question: Would she really rather die than love me again?

Jules looks away, turning her head to the side even as I grip her nape tighter. I pull back slightly, forcing her to look at me.

"That would make it easy for you, wouldn't it?" I ask, hearing my own voice crack. I nip her earlobe with my teeth and wait a moment for her to answer, but all I can hear is the combined sound of our heavy breathing. "It would be so easy to hate me if I were the monster you want to believe I am." I struggle with how true my words are. "If I wasn't the man you fell in love with, but I am."

I kiss the side of her neck, my fingers trailing along her

skin and pulling her sleep shirt up slowly. My body's so close to hers but I don't touch her, because I want her to feel my absence. I want her to crave how I make her feel.

I trail the words down her neck, whispering against her skin. "All I want is for you to remember how much I love you and how much you love me."

I want her to beg for my touch again, just like she did when we first met. I know she will. She needs me just as much as I need her. "Give me one month." I speak without thinking, desperate for a change between us. "One month of just pretending. Of trying to forget or forgive and going back to what we once had."

She peers up at me with a brightness in her eyes, but they narrow with distrust. I add, "If you hate me still at the end of the month, I'll let you go." I can barely speak the pained words, but I push out the offering.

My heart beats hard in my chest, knowing it's a lie. But it's something she can hold on to. It's a deal with the devil for her, and I'm sure she knows it.

She doesn't reply, and I couldn't give a fuck so long as tomorrow things have changed for us.

My strides are heavy as I leave her to grab the ring from where it lays, once again on the floor. She stares at it rather than at me when I take her hand. "I'm the same man I was when I first put this ring on your finger." I slide the diamond on her ring finger and hold it there, waiting for her eyes to reach mine.

I lean in and breathe in her scent, closing my eyes and forcing myself to let go of her. "Don't take it off, Jules. That ring will stay on your finger." I watch as her eyes close and her chest rises. "I'll make sure of it."

ten

Julia

The mind plays tricks,
It likes to deceive.
What once brought you joy,
Will now make you grieve.
What to think, what to do,
When there's no easy way out.
When your heart's torn and broken,
And all you know is doubt.

I WISH A HOT SHOWER COULD WASH IT ALL AWAY. As if the steam and heat could cleanse the burden of knowing what Mason did nearly a year ago. So long ago, when we were both two different people. When we were both strangers to each other.

I don't know what to think, and I don't know how to react or which emotion is coming through the strongest. It makes me feel crazy. It's like the sway of the ocean. As soon as one wave comes and crashes over me, another is already waiting to drown me. It's making me weak.

It's late, but I don't want to sleep.

I move to my dresser and sift through the nightgowns mindlessly, remembering how even last night, I questioned if I should refuse him. When Mason laid his arm across my belly, turning on his side to be closer to me, I hesitated before asking him to move and let me be like I have been. It comes down to one truth: I wanted him to take the pain away. The pain he caused. Only him. He's responsible for it all. *Just the same, only he could take it away.*

Glancing down in the drawer I trail my fingers across a nightgown; it's all silk and fine lace. Tempting, luxurious and expensive. I bought new lingerie a few weeks back, for Mason of course. The shine of the navy blue silk catches my eye, but I can't bring myself to pick it up.

I don't want to tempt him anymore. I don't want to try to look beautiful for him. My heart aches with a pain that feels as if it will strangle the life from me. I wish Mason were done with me, because I already feel myself needing his touch again.

It makes me feel pathetic, but what choice do I have? I have no one and nothing, and I've been forced into a corner I can't escape.

I shut my mouth tightly, gritting my teeth as I ball up the silk gown's matching thong in my hand and slam the drawer closed.

He's not a good man. He planned my husband's murder in cold blood.

But he's damn good to me in ways my husband wasn't. If what he said was true… I take in a ragged breath before sitting on the edge of the bed, still only covered by the towel from my shower. The mattress groans as my eyes close and I lean back, collapsing on the bed.

A thought has taken over, one I least expected. I'm still angry with Jace and the more I want to believe Mason, the more I think Jace really did it. He had a woman killed.

How could I not have known what kind of man Jace was? I already know he lied to me, that he stole from me. I have evidence of that from bank account statements and the deed to the apartment he took his mistress to. *Or mistresses.* I'll never know.

If you'll lie, you'll cheat. If you'll cheat, you'll steal. If you'll steal, you'll kill.

I know for a fact Jace did two of those things. Three, technically, since he used my money and not his to buy that property.

I'm disgusted in every way possible. What's worse is that if Jace hadn't passed, maybe I never would have known. We'd still be together and I'd still be living a lie, completely blind to it all. Utterly naïve.

The reality is sickening. I do believe Mason. I believe my husband had a woman killed. But that doesn't mean moving forward I choose to be with a murderer. How could I ever trust Mason again? How could I ever look at him the same?

If only the shower could rinse it all away. Or a pill could erase my memory.

But then I'd be back to the life I once had, not knowing

a thing about the lies and corruption, all the sins I've been blind to.

Defeated but still moving forward, I mumble, "To hell with going back to that." I stretch my back as I stand up, knowing I need to get dressed for bed before Mason barges in here. I don't have the luxury of being lost in my thoughts.

One month, and then what? It's pointless to truly consider the question because I don't believe Mason will let me go. Besides, what would I do if in one month he lets me walk out the door?

I pretend that I don't know how that scenario plays out. I go back to being alone, but never trust anyone again? That's really what hurts the most, the lies and secrets make me feel as though no one is truthful. The two men I gave everything I ever had to turned out to be liars and murderers. I huff a pathetic and humorless laugh.

My girlfriends were right, I really do pick winners.

I'm only able to take two steps to the bathroom door before hearing the door at the end of the hall open. I stare at my closed door, waiting for Mason to enter, but then I hear another door open and shut only a moment later with a click that echoes down the hall.

My forehead pinches with confusion as I hear it again. It's as if someone is checking inside of each room in the hall-way. I almost call out to tell Mason that I'm in here and I'm not hiding, but something eerie stops me. A chill I've never felt before, like a grave warning from someone or something watching over me, runs down every inch of my skin and my heart races with sudden fear.

Another door opens, then closes. And this last one was closer.

All I can hear is my heart pounding in my chest as I get down on my knees as quietly as I can and crawl under the bed. *Something's wrong.* I hear the door next to the master bedroom close as I try to turn onto my side, but I can't. I'm stuck, wedged between the floor and the bed frame, but it's enough. My heart beats wildly and I try to convince myself it's just Mason and I'm being stupidly foolish again. Keeping as still as possible, I watch the door only six feet or so away, the light from the hallway faintly pouring in through the crack and shining against the gleaming hardwood.

Click. It opens softly, and two shiny black shoes walk in softly. *It's not Mason.* I know it's not. Fear fills my veins. Violently and with a chill that's paralyzing.

I can't stop the adrenaline from pumping through my blood as the shoes leave my periphery. The footsteps thud to my right, but I can't see him. I hear the bathroom door open and terror runs through me, wondering if I've left the light on. If whoever it is that's come up here will know I'm in this room.

Steam will still be on the bathroom mirror and he's going to see where I've messed the bed up from lying there just a moment ago. My heart rages so hard that I swear it's trying to leave my body. If he touches the comforter, he'll feel that it's warm. He'll know I was here only moments ago.

"Jules?" My eyes widen and flash to the open doorway as I hear Mason call for me from downstairs. I can faintly hear him walking to the bottom of the staircase, and I can practically see him standing down there. Given his casual tone, he's completely unaware there's someone else in the house.

God help me; I want to scream.

The black shoes quickly leave the bedroom but not

so quick that the man ran. His steps were silent. He gently closes the door and the click is barely heard. I'm caught between wanting to scream out to warn Mason and saving myself.

Whoever it is that was in this room a moment ago doesn't answer Mason and he doesn't go down the stairs; instead he goes to the left, farther into the house.

I didn't think it possible, but my heart slams harder as I hear Mason start to climb the stairs.

Move! my inner voice begs me. My palms are clammy against the wooden floors as I drag myself across the floor. *Do something!* I don't know who's here, I don't know what they've come for. But I can't stay here and let Mason walk into what could be his death sentence.

I crawl out as quickly as I can, the rug beside the bed burning against my forearms and the metal from the bed frame scraping against my back, but I'm out with time enough to open the door just as Mason reaches the top of the stairs. I swing the door open prepared to scream and when I do, the man is standing right there, staring at the stairwell with a gun in his hand. The thin silencer on the end is pointed straight ahead, right at where Mason should be in only a moment.

"Mason!" I yell out his name, or at least I think I do. I can't hear anything but a loud ringing and my body is so numb from fear and the heat coursing through my body that I can barely feel a thing. As if I'm not even here. As if I've left my body, yet I'm still standing where I was.

The end of the gun points straight at me, only feet away with nothing in between us.

My head spins, and my vision nearly goes black from

fear. I never imagined what it would be like to know that you're dying. That you only have a precious second or two left to live.

How time would slow and my body would sway, yet be utterly still.

As I stare at the man's cold dark eyes, it feels as if I don't even exist anymore. They're so brown, they're nearly black. His skin is a beautiful tan, but it looks pale against the black turtleneck and leather jacket he's wearing.

He doesn't look like a killer; he's too handsome, his clothes too expensive.

But that's just what he is.

I'd think this was all a nightmare, if it wasn't for the way Mason screams out and snaps me from this moment, bringing me right back as my own scream pierces my ears.

But the man doesn't shoot, and instead he turns and runs.

eleven

Mason

"No!" The word is ripped from my throat as my body moves forward purely out of instinct. My muscles scream as I move as fast as I can, watching the end of the silencer swing toward Jules.

Not my Jules. Not my sweetheart. *Take me instead.*

I lunge forward to block her, but I already know it's too late. The strike of a bullet doesn't hit me and I can barely stand to open my eyes, my body pressed to Jules, expecting the bullet to have already found her. It's her wide eyes and heavy breathing that hammer the message into my thick skull that she's all right. I search her body for any sign of an injury, but she pushes my hands away. "He's running!" she screams in my face.

He could have killed her. I saw it happen. In that split second, she was dead. It takes more than a moment to come to grips with the fact that she's still here. She's alive. She's okay. And the prick who pointed a gun at her is getting away. With his back to us, he sprints toward the end of the hall and into the last bedroom.

My muscles coil as I stand up, hell-bent on killing the bastard. "Stay there!" I scream at Jules as I chase after him, my heart pounding.

He slams the door behind him, but the palms of my hands smack against it and my shoulder shoves the door open.

It all happens so fast, I can't think, I can't control what I do. With my hands still on the door, a fist crashes into my face, catching me off guard.

My jaw cracks as my head snaps back and he lands another blow before I've recovered from the first.

I bring my fists up, ready to fight, but he shoves me back, even as I strike him hard in the shoulder. He yells out in agony but doesn't stop. The push gives him enough room to get by me. I can't let him go. He's fucking dead.

Fisting his jacket, I grab him with everything I've got, ripping at it and ignoring the shit that falls from his pocket. My nails scratch at his slacks, ripping down the fabric but I get ahold of him, tripping up his right leg and the man falls hard to the ground.

Adrenaline courses through my veins and all I can see is my fist pounding into him over and over. But then I hear her scream.

Jules cries out, terrified, and I stop to look at her, my heart leaping up my throat. I stare at her and search for the threat, the danger that's scared her. There's no threat that I can place. She stands there in the doorway, her hands over her mouth, pale with fright and looking so frail. It's only when I feel the man beneath me buck his hips, lunging with all of his strength and moving so fucking fast I can't pin him down that my attention leaves her.

"Stay in the room!" I shout at her, hating that I can't be in two places at once. Torn between protecting her by staying close, and eliminating the danger. I launch myself forward, grabbing at him once again but failing to find purchase. My muscles scream in pain as I lunge at full speed after the man I don't recognize. He swings around the banister and gets ahead of me, but I take the stairs two at a time, feeling my blood get colder and colder as I leave her behind.

Someone else could be here.

The thought makes my foot slip on the last stair. My heel catches the edge and I fall forward. I'm so close to him though that when I reach out for him, I pull him back by closing my fist around his sweater. I reach up with my other hand, ready to wrap my arm around his throat, ready to pull his body to my chest and hold him there until the struggling stops.

I'll strangle him until he has no life left.

But he's quicker and has better balance than I do, slipping the thin leather jacket off and tearing for the door.

It's unlocked. It's never unlocked. It wasn't earlier. Not a damn soul has a key other than me.

The door stays wide open as he disappears from view. The jacket flies behind me as I follow after him. The harsh and brutal wind wraps around every inch of my heated skin.

I'm only a few feet behind him, but he's running faster and with every step I'm reminded that I'm leaving her farther and farther behind.

Someone else could be there. You can't leave her alone.

The man darts to the right, gaining ground and slipping from my vision behind the row of trees. *Fuck!* I can't think straight with thoughts of her.

Closer to the street, the sound of cars passing parallel to us surround me as I sprint after him, but it's useless. I can't see a damn thing through the pine trees. I keep running even though I don't see him. I don't stop even when the cars flying by lay on their horns.

Where the fuck did he go? There's nowhere to hide. I stand on the curb, listening to the cars whizzing by only feet away and searching everywhere. I spin around to my right and left trying to find the man, but he's vanished.

Another car beeps several times as the cold sinks in, and I realize I'm not even wearing shoes. My bare feet sink into the thin layer of snow and my heavy breath fogs in front of my face.

Jules.

Her name echoes in my head as I race back to the house, breathing in the cold air and letting it soothe my tired lungs.

The vision of her staring down the silencer of the gun is the only thing I can see as I ignore the harsh weather, and the screaming of my aching muscles as I run with everything I have back to the house.

The warmth of the house is anything but calming. It's too eerie. Too quiet. I barely hold onto the banister as I fly up the stairs, terrified I've played into this fucker's hand. That he outsmarted me. That he came back for her. I don't know who he is. I don't know how he got in here. All I know is that he was here, and he was going to kill her.

I don't stop moving until I'm upstairs. I just need her here, I need her to be safe.

"Jules!" I cry out before I shove the bedroom door open.

"Mason," she whimpers. She's worried and terrified, but she runs straight to me, burying her head in my chest and clinging to me.

"Thank fuck," I whisper into her hair, holding on to her just as tight. Her chest meets mine and she's pressed against me like she can't get close enough. I stroke her damp hair with my cheek, leaving soft kisses and rubbing her back over and over.

She's okay. Thank fuck she's here. I close my eyes, but the moment I do, the fucker's face flashes into my mind.

Who is he? And why the fuck was he here?

The answers come easily, making my grip on Jules tighten.

A hitman. Here to kill. Because he was hired to do just that.

"My father is a dead man." It's all I can say. "I'll kill him for this." My throat scratches with a rawness of pain that touches the very marrow of my bones. Jules pulls away from me, sniffling and looking up at me with a look I can't make out in her eyes.

She doesn't answer for the longest time, just staring back at me as I slowly catch my breath. *I'm so sorry, Jules.* The apology is trapped at the back of my throat.

"He had this." Jules breaks the moment with her weakly spoken words. She holds out what she found and a chill sweeps over me. A syringe. "It fell on the floor when," she says and pauses, clearing her throat, then tucks her hair behind her ears, looking past me to the last bedroom. She swallows, wrapping her arms around her shoulders and taking a step away before finishing her statement. "When you were on him."

She doesn't look at me, she continues to back away, moving farther into the master bedroom and I follow until the back of her knees hit the bed and she sits on the edge. Is she angry with me? I miss her warmth immediately, my knuckles pulsing with pain at the memory of beating the piss out of the man who would have killed her.

"I had to, Jules."

Her eyes rip away from the ground and she stares into my own. "I know," she whispers, but the pain and sadness in her eyes won't go away. My chest rises with a heavy breath. I don't understand her reaction.

I close my fist around the syringe as I take a step closer to her. She doesn't pull away, not even when I cup her chin in my hand. "Are you okay?" I ask, staring deep into her eyes.

She nods her head and pushes her cheek into my palm. My worry leaves me when she leans into me, covering my hand with her own and closing her eyes.

"Mason," she whispers in a pained voice and it breaks my heart.

I bend down to hold her, to embrace her and tell her that everything's going to be all right. It'll never happen again.

As I get closer to her, my cell phone goes off in my back pocket.

She bites down on her lip as I rest my forehead against hers, hating that I'm being pulled away from her. I take it out from my back pocket only to silence it, to give her my full attention and make sure she knows she's safe, but I see it's my father.

"Stay here," I tell her softly.

"Where are you going?" she asks as she reaches out for me, grabbing my hand as if I'm leaving her alone in hell.

"Just downstairs," I say, letting go of her hand but not before kissing her knuckles. They're soft and undamaged, unlike my own. I look over my shoulder at her as I answer the phone and pass through the bedroom door.

"Hello," I say coldly as I shut the door and take each step of the stairs carefully. The thuds of my feet are in time with the beating of my heart, slow and meticulous.

"Mason, I have the numbers and it's going to be rough," my father says and doesn't wait for me to reply. He's in full-on business mode. As if I would buy that and this isn't damage control.

The click is loud as I lock the front door. I'm barely listening to the man ramble on the other end. He's an idiot if he thinks for one moment this call will fool me.

Dragging out the chair at the head of my dining room table, I stare at the front door, my eyes focused on the lock before flicking over to the stairs.

I can't fucking calm down being so far away from her.

She's safe, I tell myself repeatedly.

"Stop," I say into the phone, halting my father midsentence. "Do you think I don't know it was you?" My tone is menacing.

"What was me? Are you still on about the… incident?"

Rage pushes down the accusations.

"You have something and I have something. I'll be

damned if you're going to screw me on this deal, Mason. Think with your fucking head for once!" He scolds me like he used to, his anger on full display. "I thought we had a deal after I let her walk out with you. Was the understanding not clear?" There's silence after the unspoken threat.

"Attempting to have her murdered is a part of your deal?" I ask him evenly, although my pulse betrays any calmness I attempt to maintain.

"Jesus Christ, Mason! Why won't you get over it?"

"So you wouldn't hurt her? You wouldn't threaten her life?" The recent events play in my vision as the syringe in my hand taps back and forth on the table.

He snuck in. He had a syringe. He had a gun but didn't use it.

"I meant to scare her. But I..." he trails off and the strength leaves my father's voice. "I made a mistake before and maybe I am a little heavy handed, but whatever she was going to say, she didn't. You can't be angry with me for that."

"The hell I can't. And if you ever hurt her, I'll kill you." I don't bother mincing my words; we're well past thinly veiled threats. "If anything happens to her," I say as my blood runs cold as I swallow thickly before continuing, "I'll kill you myself."

All I can hear on the other line is a long exhale. "You control her, Mason," my father says and continues with business. He carries on like this conversation didn't include a threat to his life. All the while, I stare at the sharp silver needle of the syringe.

If my father didn't do this, who did?

"Something happened." My throat dries up and I lean forward, hating that I'm relying on him. Hating that I'm in such deep shit I can't get out myself. I take in a heavy breath before saying, "Someone came here."

There's a pause on the other end of the line. "Where's here? Your home?"

"Yes, someone broke in; I don't know how. Someone with a gun and he tried—"

"Are you all right?" my father asks, not letting me finish, and he sounds genuinely concerned.

"I'll be all right when he's dead," I answer him coldly, and it's the truth. "And if I find out you had anything to do with it—"

"I didn't," he says, his sharp tone meant to assure me.

I don't respond, not knowing any longer what to believe.

"Are you sure you want to discuss this over the phone?" he asks after a moment of quiet, and I already know I shouldn't. I pause, and he continues.

"Do you know who it was?" my father asks, but there's something in his voice that's off. Something that makes my blood turn cold. "Was there anything on him?" he asks me with a hint of desperation. The line is silent as I look at the syringe on the table.

"No," I say, my voice falling flat.

"Where is he?" he asks me.

I clear my throat and say, "There wasn't anything on him."

"Tell me his location, I'll take care of this. You don't have to worry—"

"He's gone!" I scream into the phone, feeling increasingly angrier.

A hitman. I only know one man who's ever hired a hitman, and he's on the other end of the phone.

The front door was locked. Someone made that bastard

a key. I was only downstairs in the office to talk to my lawyers about the separation of the business. I was preoccupied as he crept up the stairs.

My father knew about the call. He knew. My vision turns to red and even though, for a small moment, I questioned if it could be him, it has to be.

It was my father. All the logical pieces click together, fitting nice and pretty as my father's voice comes through the phone. He just happens to call when the bastard got away? I don't fucking believe in coincidences.

I stare at the syringe on my desk. An overdose of something. That's why there was no gunshot. Too messy. The gun was for protection only.

He was here to murder Jules in a clean way so that no one would know, not even me.

My father set me up. I grip the phone tighter. He tried to kill her. A dark whisper deep in the back of my head hisses, *Just like he killed your mother.*

"It was you." The words come out of my mouth as an accusation. "You're fucking dead."

"Me?" My father's voice echoes with disbelief. "You can't be serious, Mason!"

My skin feels like it's on fire; I try to contain my rage, but it's useless.

"Never," he says on the other end. "I would never hurt her. She's yours, Mason. I'm very aware of that," he tells me, and he sounds so sincere.

I don't respond, thinking. Trying to think who would want to hurt her. Or maybe me. Maybe the asshole was after me. He didn't shoot her. He could have, but he didn't. Maybe the syringe was meant for me. Maybe the man was hired by whomever left the note. For all I know, that man is the one who left the note.

"Scare her, yes. Yes I would and if she ever did anything to hurt you, she'd be there on my list, Mason. But I would tell you. It would be your call."

My father disgusts me. Just the thought of what he's done and what he's willing to do is sickening. But he's saying this wasn't his doing. If it wasn't him, I have no clue where to look next. Nothing but a note with no name and this syringe.

"Who then?" I finally say and as I do, I hear Jules's faint steps as she comes down the stairs. I turn in my seat in the dining room to watch as she walks down slowly and then freezes when she sees me.

Her large eyes plead with me, and I instantly rise to meet her.

"Upstairs, sweetheart," I tell her as my father speaks.

"Has she upset anyone? What was she at the station for? You need to be honest with me."

I place my hand on the small of her back and lead her up the stairs. Her eyes dart to the phone as my father talks, and I know she can hear.

"No, she hasn't upset anyone," I tell him. "Her going to the station was a mistake."

"Well, someone knows something, Mason." He says it like it's obvious. "What about Liam?" he asks me. "He knew we'd be having the conference about the division of the as-sets. He has a motive." Jules nearly trips on the stairs. She shouldn't be listening to this shit.

I grab her hip to keep her from falling and almost drop the phone.

"I have to call you back," I tell him, content with the fact that it wasn't my father.

Someone knows what I did, and they're after me. They may also be after Jules. Especially now that she's seen this. We both saw his face. She's woven so deeply into my mess.

My father continues speaking into the phone but his words turn to white noise, and I simply end the call. My focus is entirely on Jules.

Her grip on me is tight, and she lets me hold her as I drop the phone to the ground and simply pull her into my lap to sit on the stairs.

Maybe it's the shock, maybe it's something else.

But I don't want to let go of her.

I don't want her to let go of me either.

"I'll find out who did this, Jules," I whisper. "I'll find them, and I'll kill them."

CHAPTER
twelve

Julia

The stars are always present,
Even though we cannot see.
The clouds will block them out,
And leave us with a plea.

Sometimes it takes the darkness,
And the coldest, purest lights.
To see what's always been there,
And cherish those stars at night.

"Mason."

He's silent as he sits on the chair in the corner of the bedroom. It's a reading chair that I bought a while back and tucked into the corner of the master when I moved in with Mason. He seems to prefer it now when he's thinking about what to do. Or maybe it's when life is breaking him down to the point where he can't stand on his own any longer.

"Mason?" I call out his name, my voice soft and again he doesn't seem to hear it. There's a comfortable groove and warmth that surrounds me since I haven't moved from my spot on the bed since we came back in here after he talked with his father. Silence sits between us, with both of us letting our thoughts run wild. His chin rests in his hand and his eyes are staring straight ahead at the armoire, unblinking.

Someone attempted to kill one of us. Or at the very least, inject whatever is in that syringe… Closing my eyes, I calmly breathe out, my fingers tightening on the blanket huddled in my lap.

"Mason, please talk to me," I say, raising my voice even louder. I want to know what he knows. I can't be left in the dark. This time his gray eyes look back at me, smoldering the moment he sees me. As if I've lit a fire, and the intensity of it stops me right where I am.

The only thing I can think in this moment is that he's going to eliminate the distance between us, to push me back on the bed, to take me like he used to with that look. My breath halts and my body stays frozen, but not with fear or denial. *This is lust.* I want him to take me, to feel my body and for me to feel his. Right now I need to be held. Just like I did all those months ago when Mason first took me home.

I want to forget it all.

Mason doesn't do any of that. The chair scoots back against the hardwood floor as he rises from the corner. He walks past me leaving a trail of coldness in his wake as he stands in front of his dresser, his back to me for a long moment.

Leaning back on the bed, I attempt to push down the wave of rejection that flows through every inch of my body. A hollowness presses against my chest. Does he no longer want me?

Isn't this what I wanted not so long ago? Why does it hurt so much, why does it hurt even worse?

Mason drops to a crouch in front of the dresser, pulling out the third drawer down and not stopping until it's completely removed from the dresser.

"What are you doing?"

"You need protection when I can't be here." It takes a moment to register what he said, but only until he reaches inside the dresser where the drawer was and pulls out a case. It's thin and silver, obviously a gun case. My gaze never leaves the brushed satin metal as he carries it to the bed.

A numbness pricks its way to my fingers at the very thought of touching it. I've never shot a gun before. I haven't ever even seen one in person until today. Until the sight of one was trained on me.

I scoot back slightly and keep my eyes on Mason, ridding myself of the thoughts of the gun that was here only hours ago.

"If someone ever comes in here again, you're going to shoot them. Do you understand me?" Mason asks.

My heart races and my body heats with an anxiety that's nearly paralyzing. I don't know if I can kill someone.

"Who was that man?" I ask Mason rather than answer, but he merely flicks his eyes to mine before turning the case around and ignoring my question.

"The combination is my mother's birthday: ten, fifteen, fifty-seven." I blink up at him, waiting for more, but he simply pushes the box closer to me, rattling it to get my attention until my fingertips slide to the cold silver metal of the combination lock.

Ten. Fifteen. Fifty-seven. *Click.* The loud noise of the case opening doesn't startle me as much as I thought it would; I'm still waiting to learn who the man was and why he was here. I need to know what he was searching for and what was in that syringe.

Mason swallows thickly, opening the case and revealing a shiny handgun.

"It's a nine millimeter. It—"

"Mason," I say, cutting him off, waiting for his eyes to meet mine. "Who was that?" I ask him when I have his full attention.

"I don't know," he answers lowly, holding my gaze.

"Why..." I can't finish my sentence, my blood rushing in my ears and my body heating.

My throat goes dry as Mason gives me nothing. His expression is unchanging, and I know right then he's not going to tell me a damn thing.

I lick my lips and push the case away from me. I didn't choose this, and I don't want it.

"You need to know how to use this, Jules," Mason says, grabbing the gun by the barrel and passing it to me handle out, insisting I take it. I stare at it, but I don't really see it. Everything's a blur.

"I can't describe how absolutely terrified I was," I say, swallowing down every fear as I rush to get it all out. "Not for my own life or what was going to happen to me, or what could have happened…" Chancing a look in his eyes, I know he hears me. I know he understands what I'm saying.

I was worried he'd never come back. I was worried Mason was going to die.

"I need you to talk to me," I tell him as my eyes burn with the emotions finally surfacing. Scooting closer to him on the bed, I lean closer and plead, "I need to know what's going on." I take a steadying breath, surprised at how even my cadence is. At how strong my voice sounds although I feel as if I'm on the verge of collapsing with hopelessness.

"I don't want to tell you more than you need to know, Jules," Mason says and looks up at me with sympathy, his strength and dominance ever present. He reaches out to cup my jaw but I flinch and move away, scooting backward slightly as I shake my head.

"No, you don't get to decide that," I tell him with a voice much louder than I anticipated. A small bit of anger seeps into the firm statement.

Mason's gaze narrows, but he doesn't respond.

"I need to know." My voice cracks, and I hate that it does, but I am truly desperate and there's no way to hide that. "You need to tell me." Without a response, I lick my dry lips and shamefully look away, down at the patterned rug on the floor. I wish my voice held the strength I feel. I wish I were stronger overall. I'm trying, I'm truly giving everything I can not to be the meek woman I was raised to be and praised for being.

"You don't need to know." His answer is short but he

keeps my gaze as if he's ready to cave to me, to give me what I want. I know that look well. I only need to ask.

"I want to know, Mason," I tell him honestly. "Please," I add as I lean forward slightly, almost reaching for his hand. Almost.

With a heavy sigh, he puts the gun back into the case. He shoves it to the side and finally tells me, "I think he was a hitman. I think there's a hit out—"

"A hit?" I blurt out, not quite picking up what he's saying at first, but then the realization floods through me, along with a coldness that cracks my composure. "Someone wants to kill you?" How I have any voice at all is beyond me.

His expression softens as he shakes his head once. "It could be either of us. But I would think that the killer knew I was downstairs in the office."

"Someone tried to kill me?" I manage to get out, but then immediately have to fight back the need to vomit. The shock is just too much. "Why?" My hands shake without my conscious consent. *Someone's trying to kill me.*

"Your father?" I can only surmise it's him. "He warned me. He… he—"

"I don't think so. I think he'd rather use you to get to me than kill you."

"Then who?" The question is torn from me. "Who the hell would try to kill me if not him?"

Mason doesn't answer me.

"Mason." I whisper his name, my face crumpling with pain as I beg him, "I don't want to die." I've thought about death so much this past year, ever since Jace died. It often occurred to me that it would be so easy to just end the pain. But I don't want that. I want to live. I want to be happy. Like I was with Mason, before I found out all the lies.

"No one's going to hurt you," Mason states with finality in a voice so full of confidence, I believe him. His white T-shirt is pulled snug across his broad shoulders and as he leans forward, looking me deep in my eyes, my heart flips and everything else but him blurs around me. "I'll always protect you, Jules. I promise," he tells me. I think he's going to reach out and touch me, that he's going to kiss me and hold me in that comforting way I've grown used to. But he doesn't. He's only inches away, so close I could touch him, but the distance between us is still there and I know I only need to give my consent to let him in. To let his touch soothe the pain that's suffocating me.

"Please hold me." I hate myself in this moment for needing Mason, for forgiving him enough to give in to my own weakness and desires. I close my eyes tight, willing my conscience to go away so he can comfort me. It's not the first time I've had to do this. And the last time sent me spiraling into a darkness I couldn't control.

"I need more than that, Jules." Mason's voice is full of raw emotion for the first time since coming back in here. My eyes open slowly, feeling the sting of tears subside and something else forcing its way through me. His cold gray eyes soften and fill with vulnerability.

Mason reaches across the bed and grips the back of my head in his hand. It's large and strong and his fingers spear through my hair with a strength that forces my lips up to his. He crashes his own against mine and pushes my body back.

I don't know how to describe the rush of desire that sparks to life between us. It's like thunder and lightning all at once, right before a downpour in the middle of an open field with no shelter in sight. It's hot and drenched between us. That's what his kiss does to me. It's a natural storm that I can't stay away from.

"Mason." I moan his name as he breaks our kiss, resting his forehead against mine and breathing heavily. His warm breath fills the small space between us, but when I look up there's nothing but pain etched on his face. Does he not feel it like I do? If I could have anything right now, I'd have him in the field with me, letting the rain soak our skin.

Wordlessly, I reach up and trail my fingers along the stubble of his strong jaw.

"I thought I'd lost you," he whispers and his voice is low and carries the same agony I'm feeling. I almost tell him I know what it feels like, I almost let the tears come back, but then his lips meet mine in a soft, slow kiss that makes my heart race.

I thought I'd lost him. I thought I was going to die before that. "Just hold me," I whimper, my voice a strangled plea.

"Always," Mason murmurs before kissing me long and deep. My back hits the bed and my legs part for him. The tension blisters between us with a passion I thought was long gone. Its intensity refuses to be denied as I cling to him, every bit of me wanting to be pressed against him. He breaks the kiss and I have to tilt my head back to breathe in the cool air as he kisses down my body. Each one takes time, leaving a cool sensation behind as his hot kisses move on to the next spot. It's too slow, yet it's just right.

He takes off my clothes as he goes, slowly stripping me for him. With every moment I'm conscious of what I'm allowing him to do. Watching myself give in to baser needs and allow a man I despised to crawl down my body, holding me as if he owns me, but he does it so gently, as if I'm precious to him. I love every second of it and I know I still love him. The swarm of emotions rages, but only one wins out.

My head digs into the mattress as my neck arches and I lift my hips for him.

I may be a fool, but I know what I want and need.

He kisses just below my belly, sending goosebumps to flow across my bare skin before moving lower. I'm hot for him; my body aches for him. His heated breath causes a sweet sensation of desire to travel up my body and harden my nipples.

I let my hands slowly travel from my breasts to his hair, running my fingernails down his scalp as he pulls off the rest of my clothes and lets them drop to the floor. They fall into a crumpled heap and make the only sound that fills the room besides our breathing and the pounding of my heart.

Mason places his hands on my inner thighs and he doesn't have to push; I immediately spread them wider for him. He stares between my legs and even though my cheeks heat with a violent blush, I can't tear my eyes away from his as he leans forward and gently sucks on my clit.

I cry out my pleasure. It's instant and forceful, just as Mason is.

My legs try to close together to force him away, my fingers gripping onto his muscular shoulders and nails digging into his skin, but he doesn't let up until a wave of my orgasm rises slowly through my toes and fingers. It moves higher and higher and then crashes hard, rocking through my body without any mercy. My head thrashes to the side as I cry out, and I'm only vaguely aware as Mason kisses back up my body with purpose and need this time. He buries his head in the crook of my neck, biting down slightly as he slams himself deep inside of me. He doesn't wait for me to adjust. He only takes his pleasure from me as easily as he gave me my own, ruthlessly riding through my release.

He groans deep and low as he pounds into me over and over again. My body begs me to move, but I'm paralyzed by pleasure. By Mason.

It's fitting really. I'm held beneath him with a passion I can't fight. With a love I can't deny. I can try to fight it, but it's useless.

He braces himself on his forearms to look down at me, never relenting his powerful thrusts. My arousal leaks between us as he lowers his lips to mine.

The dim waves rise again through me, making my body shiver and the rest of me tense. It's coming fast and strong and it's inevitable, I know it is. I hold on to Mason for dear life, letting him take from me and crashing my lips into his.

thirteen

Mason

She's broken,
Shattered,
Ruined beyond repair.
The truth has destroyed her,
And left her
Choking on the air.

MY MOTHER DIED OF AN OVERDOSE.

This can't be a coincidence. It's all I keep thinking as I remember the syringe. I threw it into the fireplace and watched it burn, the thick plastic slowly melting and the liquid boiling into nothing, leaving only a thin needle in the ashes.

I couldn't take it to the police. It only took an opioid test to prove what I thought. It was heroin. It's been two days and I only have one answer to all the questions. The syringe was filled with an opioid and I imagine if the killer had done his job, I would have gone upstairs to find Jules dead of an overdose.

I readjust in my seat in the corner of the bedroom, my laptop on the nightstand I've pulled over to the chair. The dim light from the screen provides the only illumination in the dark room. My tumbler of whiskey sits next to it, but I can't drink. I can't do anything but read the report of my mother's death and let the doubt and anxiety wash through me.

For years I blamed my father.

The therapist he sent me to was under the impression she took her own life because all they did was fight and there were concerns about my mother's sudden erratic behavior. Concerns that wound themselves around whispers of drug use.

I blamed my father because I thought he did it.

He wasn't home when it happened, but that was nothing new. He was never around on the weekends. I was in my bed, but the house was so cold. The air conditioner was turned down far too low.

I remember thinking it was odd that the heat had been turned off. Our house became an icebox.

The moment I clicked it on, I heard the shower upstairs. Maybe I was waiting for the telltale sound of the heater, but until then I hadn't realized I could hear the shower.

I remember how I knocked on the bathroom door, but didn't go in at first. I waited and waited, wondering why she'd be in there so late. Wondering if she was crying again.

I only opened the door an hour later because I'd convinced myself she couldn't still be in there. Not after so long. The water had to be cold by then.

My parents' bathroom door wasn't locked. The knob turned easily and when the door opened and I didn't see a shadow behind the curtain, I was confused but relieved to discover the water had just been left on. Everything felt so off that night, like something was horribly wrong. I was genuinely relieved.

It wasn't until I pulled back the curtain that I saw her.

I slam the computer shut, willing the memory to leave me.

The vision of my mother dead, her body at an unnatural angle. The water was freezing, and it'd turned her lips blue. It didn't stop me from shaking her. From trying to make her wake up.

I screamed and cried out helplessly even though I knew we were alone. There was no one to help. I had to leave her to call the police. I couldn't though, not for a long time. I was shivering in my wet clothes by the time I ran down the stairs to call the cops. I couldn't believe she was gone, but she was limp and heavy and so cold.

It didn't take long for the police to come. Commissioner Haynes was there first.

My father took hours to arrive, though. Hours of sitting on my bed, being questioned over and over until I wasn't sure anymore what had happened.

I only knew I felt completely alone in the world.

The first thing my father said to me was, "I thought you were staying over at your friend's this weekend." No sorrow was evident. No sympathy that I'd found my mother dead in the shower.

His tone carried an accusation even. I remember staring up at him. The police moved around the house, blurring my vision as my father came into focus and the pieces clicked into place.

For years I've felt he was responsible and even now, even after he'd managed to convince me on the phone that it wasn't him, I imagine he's somehow involved.

I can't shake my gut feeling.

I want to murder him.

The thought makes me close my eyes, trying to rein in the anger from today and from all the years of second-guessing what happened to my mother.

When I open them, they've adjusted to the darkness and I stare at my phone.

I've asked him, but he's a liar. I already know he's capable of murder.

Everything in me is telling me it's my father who hired that man and possibly left the note to scare Jules off before deciding to kill her. I have no other leads.

The person who left a note had different handwriting than his though, more feminine. Perhaps he has a partner or maybe he hired someone but who would he trust?

The only other enemy I have is Liam. He's married, but I can't see it being him and having his wife involved. And Liam wasn't around when my mother died.

I run my hand down my face, feeling exhaustion weighing down on me, but not wanting to sleep. I can't. I'm too afraid to take my eyes away from Jules. My guard refuses to go down for even a second.

I know she hasn't forgotten everything and that maybe the other night, the moment we shared, was a mistake in her eyes. It kills me just to imagine her thinking of it as if that's all it was. A mistake.

The sound of her stirring on the bed and the accompanying slow movements catch my attention. A soft sound of pain carries through the air, and I rise to see if she's all right.

She turns on her side, pulling the sheet between her legs and letting it fall off her gorgeous curves. I brush her hair from her face, leaning down to kiss her gently on the cheek, loving how she can't fight me in her sleep.

When I pull back, her long lashes flutter open and she looks up at me. At first there's a softness to her expression, like the way she used to look at me. But it quickly changes, the trace of a smile dimming as her memories come back to her.

Her shoulders tense and she turns her head, but she doesn't push me away, even as I run my hand down to her waist and sit next to her on the bed.

The bed protests as I climb in under the sheet, still in my white undershirt and flannel pajama pants. I sigh heavily, feeling exhaustion desperately try to force me to sleep as I rest my head on the pillow and pull Jules close to me.

Just like earlier this week, she lets me hold her. She doesn't hold me back, though. Her hand merely rests against my chest, her head on my shoulder. Still, I'll take it. The feel of her small body pressed to mine, the faint sounds of her breathing and the way she nestles her head down against me, brushing the hair from her face is everything to me.

"Talk to me, Jules," I say softly. I miss her. I miss the banter and her optimistic energy. I miss her stories and the sweet sound of her laughter. "I miss you," I confess.

"I'm not sure if we're okay," she says quietly, as if it's a reminder to herself. "There are parts of you that scare me."

I tell her, "But not all of me."

Her eyes are wide open but staring across the room. I readjust my shoulders on the pillow, keeping my arm around her and debating what to tell her. She's quiet for a long time but then she asks, "You said Jace had a woman killed?"

I can only nod.

She's silent, obviously waiting for me to continue.

"I didn't know him well, but he was…" I pause to take a deep breath and stare at the mirror across the room. In the reflection I can see the top of Jules's head resting on my chest. Her eyes are vacant, as if she's broken. Not the woman I once knew, not the Jules I fell in love with. She's not running from me, as if this new woman has become resigned to her fate.

"I saw him for a meeting, and it was the only time I met him," I tell her. I want to explain and I pray she understands.

She shifts on my chest and I splay my hand on her back to keep her close to me, to keep her from moving away, but I don't have to. She's only readjusting and she stays with her cheek pressed against my chest as she pulls the sheet up higher.

"I did it," I say, feeling the words dying to come out of me. To tell her the truth. To tell her how angry he made me. How Jace was so sure of himself, so happy with what he'd done. "Her life was meaningless to him."

"Whose? Whose life?" Jules brings her hand back toward herself, retreating slightly but I reach out to grab it. I bring her fingers to my lips and slowly kiss each knuckle. She doesn't look at me while I do, but when I set her hand back down, she leaves it there.

I don't know what to make of her in this moment. Maybe she's numb, but she's receptive. She's lost her fight to deny it all.

"Her name was Avery."

Jules shifts uncomfortably as she says the words before I can. "She was his mistress?"

I nod my head as I say, "I knew her as well." It's the gentlest way I can put it.

"You *knew* her?" Jules asks in a tight voice. It's the loudest she's spoken for this conversation.

"I did," I answer honestly. "Obviously it was before we met. Before I knew you."

She nods her head into my chest and whispers, "Why?"

"Why did he want to kill her?"

My question forces her expression to fall even farther, but she nods.

"She was pregnant," I tell her and that's the last straw for Jules's composure. I hold her close as she tries to turn away. I kiss her shoulder as she hunches over and tries to hide her face from me.

"It's okay," I whisper into the tense air between us. The hurt and betrayal are echoed in her ragged breaths. I can only imagine how much it shredded her to hear the words, because it killed me to say them to her.

She pushes her hands against my chest slightly, and I let her go for a moment.

Sitting up as if searching for more air, she pushes the thick sheet off of her and pulls her long brunette hair over her shoulder as she scoots up the bed and readjusts herself to lean against the headboard. All the while I can see her reining in the emotions, hiding it all and shoving it down. But she's swallowed the truth of it all: her husband wanted his mistress dead because she was pregnant. It will stay with her forever.

"Was the baby..." she starts to ask in a choked voice as

she lies back next to me and instantly places her head on my chest. "Whose was it?" she asks.

My heart clenches in my chest, hating that I have to answer her and knowing it's going to torture her. "His," I finally answer.

She nods once, letting me know she acknowledges what I've just told her, but she's silent. A long time passes with neither of us saying anything. My fingers trail up and down her arm, moving to the dip in her waist and back up her body again. Her breathing becomes steadier, deeper and so does mine. Slowly, she gets comfortable alongside me again, resting down in bed, but neither of us sleeping.

"Did you love her?" she asks just as my eyelids feel so heavy I could fall asleep, her fingers gripping onto my shirt but still she doesn't look at me.

"No. I've never loved anyone like I love you," I tell her and then realize she may not believe me. It's true, though. I'd never planned on spending my life with someone. I didn't think it possible for someone who carries the demons that drag me down. But now I can't see my life without Jules in it. She's a bright light to my darkness. The only hope I've ever had is in her hands.

Again, she acknowledges me with only a small nod.

"Can you forgive me?" I ask her quietly, almost too afraid of her answer to even utter the word *forgiveness*.

Time passes and I think she may have fallen asleep, but then her shoulders shake with a small sob.

"No," she says and my chest sinks from her admission but also from the raw pain in her voice. "You didn't have to murder him." She adds, nearly choking on her words, "But I believe you." She sniffles once and it's then I feel her tears soaking into my shirt. She brushes her cheek against my shirt and settles back down against me.

She believes me, and that's a start.

She needs me, and she's clinging to me because she has nowhere else to go.

At least I can hold her for a little while, but even with her so close to me, even with this progress, I feel farther away from her than I've ever been.

CHAPTER
fourteen

Julia

It's absurd to move through life,
When there's nothing left inside.
When you're hollow and unfeeling,
When all you know has died.

Numb to touch, numb to move,
And silent with no voice.
But strength comes in the darkest times,
When you no longer have a choice.

RAUD. I KEEP HEARING THE WORD OVER AND over in my head. There's no way I can do this. No way I can stand in front of a room full of people, this hollow shell of a woman, and smile as if nothing has changed. There's no way I can laugh and play along with the façade of a happy couple deeply in love.

They'll see through me; I know they will.

I've always been acutely aware of my public persona. My mother used to tell me it was important for the family name. All my life I've known how to hide behind a beautiful face and stay polite even when offended. I know just what to say, and how to act.

But right now? This moment? No. I can't go through with it. I can't pretend anymore. Pretending's what got me into this mess.

"You look beautiful." Mason's deep baritone voice sends a thrill through my body. His approval always has, and my natural instinct is to cling to him right now. I want to hide behind him. He could make everything all right or at least that's the way it would feel.

Even more than that, I so desperately care for him despite everything that's happened, and that's what's breaking me.

"Thank you," I whisper and then clear my throat, turning my gaze back to the entrance of the Regency Auditorium as the limo stops in front of the building, my fingertips haphazardly grazing the crystals on my dress with nerves that won't be tamed.

I used to live for this. All the gorgeous gowns and flowing champagne, the photographs and mingling. Now instead of desire and excitement and anticipation, all I feel is dread.

I turn back to Mason just as he places his large hand over mine, and in that moment I remember who he is and what he's done and why everything has changed. I want to pull away. My body and mind are confused. I feel attacked and cornered, but I don't know who to blame other than myself.

"It's going to be all right. You're fine," Mason tells me. His voice is a soothing balm, but it's a lie. A sweet, pretty lie meant to calm me down so I can do as I'm told and act appropriately.

Pulling my hand away from him, I watch his face fall and the divider rolls down slowly; it's the only sound in the cabin.

"Is this all right, Mr. Thatcher?" Marcus, the driver, asks. I can't look him in the eye. I swallow thickly, watching the sparkling gowns flow by as women walk past. I know many of them, or at least recognize their faces. Tonight is a fundraiser for diabetic children. Nearly three hundred people will be in the grand ballroom, bidding on donations lined with spotlights and making small talk while sipping champagne and gossiping or bragging.

It's how these functions run. Who you know and who you talk to can be different, so long as you're seen with each group of individuals accordingly.

My role has changed from socialite sweetheart who brings the press to that of devoted arm candy. The to-do list hasn't changed, though: look pretty, smile and be charming. It didn't seem so bad all these years I've been doing this. Even my father used to bring me to events like this as a teen. I loved it. I was proud to come and be a part of the social scene especially when they involved causes like this one.

"This is fine," Mason answers Marcus and I grip my Chanel clutch as if it will protect me and save me from having to walk out there. "I'll open her door; thank you."

"I don't know that I'm ready," I whisper to Mason, turning to him and leaning in, acutely aware that Marcus is watching. I don't have to look up to see his eyes in the rearview mirror assessing the situation to know he's taking it all in. Everyone is always watching.

Mason searches my face for something, and then the corners of his lips twitch as he reaches his arm around my waist and pulls me in closer to him.

His strength and heat and proximity all make my blood temperature rise, and the anxiety and fear are replaced with something else entirely.

"You're definitely ready," Mason says before leaning into me for a kiss. A split second passes before I even question it. It feels so natural, as if I'm the one who intended for it to happen.

As if nothing ever happened. As if the envelope had never been opened and this part of the tale ceased to exist.

I pull away suddenly, sucking in the hot air and pushing back against the leather seat. My eyes flicker to the mirror as I regain my composure, to Marcus's ever-prying view and immediately the divider begins to move back into place, granting us privacy.

Mason's hand splays on my back before I can move any farther. "Please stop," I say. He must know what he's doing to me.

"Stop what?" he asks as if he doesn't know that his kindness is worse than anything else. That craving his affection only makes me hate myself more.

I look up through my lashes, not bothering to face him as I hold the clutch tighter with both hands.

"I can't do this, Mason," I blurt out with my voice low and pleading. "I can't pretend."

He rests his hand on the back of my neck, gripping my nape but running his thumb back and forth ever so gently. Each action sends mixed signals, and that's the very crux of my position.

"You could ignore me all night," he suggests with a sad smile. "It would be better if you did that… if we were to split in a month anyway. Wouldn't it?"

His words are accompanied by a shadow, the night already darkening. Three weeks. I don't correct him, but it's three weeks that are left, not a month. Swallowing thickly, I glance at the entrance rather than entertaining his suggestion.

"Either way," he continues, "we have to attend. We can't appear to be hiding and no one is going to hurt you here."

The lights from the massive crystal chandelier just inside the auditorium's foyer sparkle and blur in a beautiful dance as two more couples enter. I ignore it and stare at the shrubbery that's barely visible.

It hurts to hear him plan a split between us. I didn't think his compromise, promise, whatever it was, was even a real possibility. Yet here he is, speaking it into existence.

Mason opens his door and leaves me without another word. I simultaneously fear him and love him, but worse, I hate myself for having any emotion toward him other than revulsion knowing he's a murderer. That's what I can't get past. It's easy to put a smile on your face and be what everyone else wants you to be when you know who you are and you're happy as that person. When you have faith in yourself.

I've lost that. It's a new low that's left me shattered and scattered into small pieces on the floor. I don't even know where to start picking them up. I only know the sharp edges will leave me bleeding out as I do.

Cool air drifts into the limo and the light shines just a bit brighter as Mason opens my door. With the wind comes his scent, a natural masculine scent mixed with a clean fragrance from his cologne.

"Don't deny me, sweetheart," Mason says just under his breath as I stare at his outstretched hand. His statement makes my eyes lift to his and I get lost in his swirls of gray and silver. I never had a chance with this man. A tortured soul lies behind those eyes that makes me weak for him. He needs love so desperately; he needs someone, and my very soul craves his.

He was my downfall. Created to destroy me. I slip my hand into his, comforted by the warmth as he wraps his fingers slowly around mine and supports me as I rise from the limo. I keep my eyes down and don't look forward. I can hardly focus on breathing as my heels click on the pavement and Mason leads me forward.

I pull my black bolero shrug tighter around my shoulders and attempt to hide from the harsh weather while ignoring everyone around me.

The doors open and the mix of chatter and the soft melody of an orchestra carry through the air and envelop me as though it's home, as though it's safe. But I'm very much aware that I'm in danger. I scan every face for the one I saw only days ago. The man holding a gun.

At the thought I grip Mason's hand tighter and he pulls me in closer to him, walking in time with me, our steps in unison as the lights get brighter and the air warmer. A small smile slips onto my face, although inside I'm screaming.

I'm dying from the hypocrisy, but intensely aware it's my only chance of survival.

"Mason," I hear a man call out and my smile falters only slightly as my steps are halted. We're to be seen. Unwaveringly present.

"Father," Mason says tightly and I stand there with a sweetness in my composure, tilting my head slightly as the breeze from the doors being opened again sends a chill up my back. My shoulders shudder and Mason wraps his hand around my hip, pulling me in closer.

I don't flinch when his father looks at me. In a crisp suit complete with a charming smile, he appears to be an entirely different man than the one I met before.

"Miss Summers, you look utterly breathtaking this evening," his father says and naturally my smile widens. It's a shame a man like him can possess such poise and charm. I suppose everyone needs some way to survive and thrive.

My heart beats faster and my limbs scream at me to run, or worse, slap the bastard across the face for what he did only days ago, but instead I part my lips and respond sweetly, "I'm so sorry for the other day. I'm afraid I wasn't well."

He falters, the real emotions showing through and just when I think he's going to hide it, when I think the mask that slipped will be forced back into place, he leans in slightly and says, "I do apologize as well," and I swear it seems sincere. "I had no right to come between you two."

Mason stiffens beside me, and my own composure threatens to dissolve. I've never faced this kind of mastery of manipulation before. I don't know whether to react sincerely or how to play this game.

"I only want what's best for my son."

It's only then that I realize our games are different. I'm no match for him, but in the same vein, he's no match for me.

"Champagne?" a server asks on my right, breaking the moment and I instantly turn to her.

"No, thank you," spills from my mouth easily and she's quick to move on after the men each shake their heads.

I watch from my periphery as she leaves, walking easily without a care and holding the tray just so. The champagne doesn't even seem to move; she's learned to do her job well.

"Excuse me a moment, Mason," I tell him, patting his forearm and waiting for him to release my hand. He doesn't, though.

He holds me a moment longer than he should, quietly watching me and waiting for a reason. "I need to use the restroom," I whisper to him as softly and flirtatiously as I can, feeling the number of eyes on us grow. It may all be in my head, because for all I know I'm losing it, and with every second my anxiety grows.

"Of course," he says although the reflection in his eyes is something else. Something far more vulnerable and unwilling. He kisses my hand, bringing it to his lips and then releasing me without another word.

I force a smile to stay in place although it begs to fall. Everything in me is screaming that something is wrong. I walk as quickly as I can to the back of the room, deeper and deeper through the crowd of beautiful guests. I turn my body slightly when needed and ignore the conversations around me as I head to the restrooms.

I could just run. I could run away.

Away from all of this, and never stop.

I'll find myself again, but not here. Not when I know I want the very thing that will bury me.

CHAPTER

fifteen

Mason

So close to having everything,
So close to nothing at all.
The teeter-totter rocks back and forth,
While knowing you will fall.

It's all there within your grasp,
But the life has turned to stone.
You should have known, you foolish man,
You were meant to live alone.

"I APPRECIATE THE APOLOGY," I TELL MY FATHER, although my gaze isn't on him at all. My eyes are on Jules's back as her hips sway and she leaves me. When I first laid eyes on her, she blended in so easily. Each small motion was seemingly genuine. Not tonight.

My sweetheart is obviously full of hurt and pain and insecurity. In a room full of fake assholes brimming with confidence and arrogance, my Jules doesn't belong.

I wonder if everyone else in this room can see it as clearly as I do. I was wrong to bring her. I could have found another way. My father's voice interrupts my thoughts. "Miss Harrington will be there, and she made it clear she's interested."

Marcy Harrington's an investor who likes to get close with her clients and "know" them before writing a check with her family inheritance. Promiscuous would be a kind word to use. In addition, she's practically untouchable, and always gets what and who she wants.

"This is about appearances, not business. I couldn't give two shits about business right now."

"Appearances?" my father asks, and I feel my hands clench at my sides. He knows damn well what the papers are saying.

"I'd like the world to know that I'm not beating her behind closed doors."

My father shrugs as if the rumor swirling around the city isn't a concern in the least. "I'd like to know what you are doing behind closed doors. Or more importantly… what's being said between you two," he says, turning his body to follow my gaze. She's vanished though, wherever she's gone.

As my eyes drift back to him, I feel the accusations rise.

Now's not the time or place, I think over and over as my forehead furrows and I shove my hands into my pockets to keep from grabbing him. My muscles are tense, and the words are on the tip of my tongue.

There's no use in letting them out though, because I know he'll just lie. He's damn good at it and so used to it, I doubt he knows the truth from a lie anymore.

"We should have a meeting soon," I say easily, completely at odds with my true feelings. "Business and otherwise."

My father's brows raise slightly, and he looks genuinely surprised. "Of course," he says, patting me on the back. "I trust it's about the matter from the other night?" he asks although it's said as a statement.

"It is," I say, feeling the ball of rage grow larger, getting harder to contain. I clear my throat and glance back to where Jules disappeared, only to see her good friend and editor Katerina striding toward me.

My face stays neutral, with no emotions expressed whatsoever as she approaches.

"I'll talk to you soon," my father says beneath his breath, turning his back to Kat and walking away without waiting for me to acknowledge him.

Kat approaches me with an expression of distrust, an air about her that makes it obvious she's here because she hasn't heard from Jules. I thought about responding to her messages myself. Jules received texts from so many people feigning concern, but really wanting gossip. And then her friends, who seem genuinely worried.

Before she stops in front of me, I force a small smile to my lips, one that's welcoming. I'm already losing my sweetheart; I need to play this right.

"Mason." Kat states my name as if she's ready for a fight, but that's not how this is going to go down. She just doesn't know it yet.

"I'm so happy you're here, Kat," I say and nod my head slightly. "Have you seen Jules already?" I play up the concern in my own voice and expression, and watch as her anger slips and her forehead pinches. She finally looks behind her for only a moment before turning her attention back to me.

"We just got here. She's here?"

"You came with Evan?" I ask her. Her husband is well known in the public relations industry, although he travels with an entirely different sort of social circle. The industry has treated him well, but he's rarely home. That's the angle I have. Two couples; the men friends, the women friends. She'll trust me. She'll help me. At least I pray she will.

"I did," she says and peers to her right, closer to the entrance before clearing her throat and adding, "He's here somewhere." She licks her lips and squares her shoulders, remembering what she's come here to yell at me about.

I cut her off before she can begin by saying, "I'd really like it if you could talk to Jules." Jules's name on my lips and the thought of someone talking to her privately makes apprehension creep into my veins at the possibility of her spilling the truth. I shrug it off and use the intensity of the truth to help create the lie. "She's taking the wedding situation a little bit hard."

Kat watches me for a moment, her eyes narrowing as she assesses my words. I lean forward, dropping my voice and letting the insecurity that is all too real show. "She's not okay," I tell her. "She could really use a friend right now."

"I haven't spoken to her in over a week," Kat says,

confiding in me and I don't let on that I know it's uncommon for Jules not to return a call. I play my emotions as I should.

"I'm not sure she *wants* to talk about it"—I can see Kat's objection on the tip of her tongue and I say it before she can—"but she needs to."

Kat's mouth stays parted and she tilts her head, still judging my request as her husband walks up behind her.

"Evan." I pull back from Kat and press my lips into an acceptable smile. One that reflects my unease for what Jules is going through. At least that's what it shows Kat. A part of me feels like a prick, like the manipulative asshole I am, undeserving of Jules. But I already knew I wasn't good enough for her, and this show, this front, is all to save us. To save what we have.

"Thatcher, how are you, man?"

A huff of a grunt leaves me as I rock back on my heels and shove my hands in my suit pockets. "That's my father's name," I say jokingly and Evan laughs deep from his chest, raising a tumbler of amber liquid to his lips. The ice clinks in his glass as he wraps his arm around his wife's waist.

"You two make quite the couple," I say, complimenting them. They have definitely been the talk of the city on more than one occasion.

"Speaking of couples," Evan says, and his cuff slips back over his wrist as he lowers the whiskey, hiding the sleeve tattoo. His left arm is covered in tattoos. His background is perfect for his profession. He's from Brooklyn with the reputation of a man who grew up on the wrong side of the law. He made a name for himself, but only in the best of ways for his job.

He never got caught. Never had a conviction, and he knows the ins and outs of the press.

That's the kind of man the industry wants representing their clients when they're out of the spotlight. Someone to party with and respect and be genuine friends with. But someone who knows when to leave the scene before it gets too rough, what to tell the press and who to go to when shit goes down.

He's damn good at what he does, but how the two of them have stayed married, I have no idea.

"Where did Jules go?" Kat interjects before her husband can finish his thought. He glances at her from the corner of his eye and then releases her, taking a sip of whiskey and looking past me as Kat steps forward. She has no idea how she's affected him.

"Just to the restroom," I say and motion to the back with my chin.

"How's she been?"

"I think she's really taking this transition hard… moving on and getting married again." I could choke on the words.

"I'm sorry to hear that." Evan's condolences are sincere, but I'm more than certain he doesn't want a part in this conversation.

"You better be good to her," Kat says, the declaration sounding like a threat.

I turn my attention back to her. "I'll take care of her, I promise," I assure her, meeting her prying gaze. I can see the moment my lies slip into place and Kat reaches up to give me a quick hug.

"I'll talk to her," she says firmly, nodding her head and giving me a sympathetic look.

"Thank you," I say and hide the fact that dread is slowly consuming me. Jules was willing to tell the police before. Her dear friend who's concerned for her well-being… I'm certain she'll tell her something.

Julia

M Y BODY GETS HOTTER AND HOTTER WITH EACH step I take. Leaning against the counter, I listen to the water rushing from the faucet; it fills the empty restroom with white noise. *Just breathe. Just breathe.* I've never wanted to run so badly. That's all I can think about.

My heels click as I walk casually out of the side exit, smiling as best as I can although I'm not meeting the eyes of any of the guests who are having quiet conversations in the hall. As they sip on their cocktails and throw their heads back in jovial laughter, I want to walk faster; my body begs me to run. It takes great effort to keep my pace easy and pretend that nothing's wrong as I tuck my hair back and say thank you to the doorman when I head outside.

Goosebumps prickle along my skin as the bitter cold greets me. I pull the shrug tighter and maintain my composure when the look from the young man holding the door is riddled with questions.

It's too cold for me to be outside without a coat; I'm certain that's what he's thinking. But I cling to my clutch, the beaded fabric nearly slipping from the sweat on my hands.

My heart races and all I can hear is the blood rushing in my ears as the door closes behind me. The dark night lays before me, the busy street only a block away and through a small alley.

This exit isn't meant for departing guests. It's meant for smoking and the faint smell gets stronger as I take a few steps farther out into the night. Away from the gala, from the spotlight and from Mason.

Glancing to my left purely out of instinct from knowing someone's there incites shock and fear both. Liam Olsen stares back at me. He pushes off of the wall, exhaling a puff of smoke that mixes with the fog of his breath. The bright red and orange embers of the cigarette travel through the air as he walks toward me. His oxford shoes crunch the snow beneath his heavy steps.

I turn to face him, my eyes flitting between him and the exit I've just left. I'm not sure anyone can see me from here. There's no light, only darkness where I've gone.

The moonlight makes Liam's skin look pale and his eyes dark as he walks closer to me. I swallow the dread in my throat and greet him accordingly. "How are you, Mr. Olsen?" My skin feels numb with the cold, yet alive with fear. I've never actually met the man, but I know the business he had with Mason dissolving has left its mark on him.

"Where's Mason?" Liam asks harshly, tossing his cigarette to the side where it's instantly extinguished by the wet snow. Smoke billows from his nostrils as he comes closer, close enough to get a glimpse of his eyes. They're nearly bloodshot and his walk uneven, but his question is forceful. I'm not sure if he's drunk or angry. Maybe both.

"Whatever happened between you two…" I can't finish the thought.

My voice is caught in my throat for a moment, my eyes going back to the exit where I can clearly see the guests. My heart pounds once then twice as time seems to pass in slow motion and I have to think quick. Liam takes a large step forward, closing the distance between us and I instantly take one back, although it's on the edge of the sidewalk and my heel slips. I almost fall backward, and he catches me.

He chuckles and reeks of liquor. I push my hands against his chest as I find purchase on the sidewalk, turning my body so he's no longer between me and the exit.

He's drunk and he's angry, so I'm careful as I pry his hands off me as respectfully as possible and desperately try to put more space between us.

"He's coming," I tell Liam breathlessly. I have to clear my throat and repeat myself to sound surer of what I'm saying, but it doesn't fool Liam. Either that, or he doesn't care.

"You really want a man like that?" he asks me. "After what he's done?" he says and squints his eyes, and my throat closes with fear with the tone he takes. *What does he know?*

"What?" I say, licking my lips although in the cold air it only makes them feel chapped. "What exactly did he do?" I ask Liam, taking another step back. I watch as he looks toward the door and then takes another step closer to me, his hands slipping into the pockets of his slacks. "Business partnerships don't always—"

"I'm going to make him pay," he says, cutting me off and raising his brow as he reaches in his pocket for something. I involuntarily tense up, but it's only a pack of cigarettes. He takes one out, then offers the pack to me as he slips a cig between his lips and tilts his head back.

"No thank you," I tell him, "I was just heading inside."

"No you weren't," he says as he lights the cigarette, the tiny flame illuminating his face. He takes the cigarette out of his mouth, pinching it between his forefinger and thumb as he says, "You just came out here."

"I made a mistake." I'm quick to answer and it only makes him smile.

"Yeah you did," he says and the smile morphs from cocky to something else. Something sinister.

"I have to go," I say and turn my back to him, heading for the door. But I only take a single step before his hand is wrapped around my hip, pulling me backward and into his hard chest.

"Get off me!" I yell out and drop my clutch as I try to pry his fingers away from me. He's holding me with a bruising force, the tips of his fingers digging into the flesh at my hips.

"Hey now," Liam says, nearly laughing the words as he spits out the cigarette and covers my mouth with his other hand. "Hush, hush, it's okay," he whispers against the shell of my ear. The cocktail of smoke and lingering alcohol mixes and fills my lungs as I heave in a breath. This is not happening.

I yank my elbow back with everything I have and shove it into Liam's gut. He releases me and I don't waste a second, I run for the door straight in front of me. My shrug falls off and I've already lost my clutch, but as far as I'm concerned, it can stay wherever it is forever.

My palms slap against the glass door, forcing my body to come to a halt and the doorman looks at me with complete surprise as I stand there doubled over and desperate for air.

I'm shaking and completely wrecked. I've dealt with drunken men and roaming hands before. But never from a man angry with my supposed fiancé. I can barely wrap my head around what happened. He grabbed me. He held his hand over my mouth.

The door opens and even though I feel like I'm going to be sick, I walk in, trying to hide what's happened, but completely unable to compose myself. My legs are shaky and I still struggle to come to terms with being grabbed like that. I don't know what to do. I grip onto the man's arm and try to clear my head from the fog of shock, but I'm not given long before a strong grip pulls me away from him.

I yell out in surprise and fear until I realize it's Mason. He holds my forearms and forces me to look at him, and I lose it.

"Jules?" He says my name, compassion and worry evident. I shake my head, and say the only thing I can think of. "Liam—" I say but then my voice croaks, unable to get out the rest of the words. Unable to express what just happened moments ago.

Tears leak from the corners of my eyes, and his concern turns to anger. I can't say for certain what he was going to do, but there's not a chance he didn't know I was scared. He knew he crossed a boundary. "He… he—"

Mason releases me quickly, slamming his arm into the door and forcing it to fly open as I nearly fall to the gleaming marble floor.

"Jules!" I hear Kat call my name from behind me. I hear the commotion around us. I can see from the reflection in the glass a crowd's come to watch.

I can't respond, I can't even turn to her or form a single thought concerning all of them.

Even as she pulls me to stand straighter and puts her face close to mine, grabbing onto me and trying to get my attention, I can't give it to her. All I can do is watch Mason disappear and wish he'd just come back. *I need him.*

Kat grips my face with both her hands and forces me to look at her. I stare into her worried eyes and confess in a ragged breath, "I'm not okay."

CHAPTER
seventeen

Mason

Anger cannot be denied,
It cannot be contained.
Carnal sins and violent ways,
Its brutality cannot be chained.

It's passion that drives the fist,
It's fear that leaves the cage.
Every movement desperate,
Pain seeping through the rage.

EVERY HOT BREATH TURNS TO WHITE FOG IN front of my face, and it pisses me off. It obstructs my view of the bastard standing right in front of me. His back is to me as he taps a carton of cigarettes against his palm.

He should have run while he had the chance.

"Liam," I call out, my chest rising and falling, my lungs filling with ice-cold air.

Knowing him, he'd fucking love for me to make a scene. I'm sure I'm playing right into his hand, and I don't give a damn.

He's drunk and looks high. His suit's disheveled as he turns to me with a half-cocked smile on his lips.

"Don't you ever fucking touch her!" I say as I walk forward and get closer to him. I have no intention of talking. I don't need to find out what happened or why. All I know is that she was terrified. And the only thing she could say was his name.

He's a dead man.

"How do you know what she came out here for?" he asks with a smirk, and I swing my fist as hard as I can into his pretty-boy smile.

I grab his collar, using it to hold him still as I hammer my fist into his face over and over again.

I smash my knuckles against his cheekbones, his nose, his mouth, the skin splitting open on contact. At first he shoved against me, a pathetic attempt to push me away. He doesn't stand a chance.

I can feel her slipping away, and I'm so fucking desperate to hold on to her. I clutch his throat, forcing him still.

My teeth grit against one another as adrenaline pumps

in my blood. *Crack!* His nose breaks as my knuckles collide with his face and I lose my hold on him. The back of his head slams into the ground. I don't stop, I can't. All I can see is red. I lower myself to the ground but he gets in a punch, surprising me. His fist crashes against my cheek and whips my head to the side.

I barely feel it. The taste of metallic hot blood fills my mouth, but that doesn't stop me either. All it does is fuel me.

"She's mine!" I scream out and Liam's eyes widen with fear. I must sound crazy. Even to my own ears, the words I yell out are those of a madman. The worst part, the most sickening, is that I don't care. Maybe I have lost it. Maybe I am crazy when it comes to Jules. I'm perfectly fucking fine with that.

I yank him up by the collar, my knees sinking into the freezing snow and the thick silk fabric of my suit pants slowly absorbing the melting snow. He slams another fist into my face, so low on my chin he nearly catches my throat, and I return the blow by headbutting his nose.

He screams out in pain and I drop him to the ground.

My breathing is erratic, my vision blurred. I know I've won, but I can't stop because never in my life has it been more apparent than seeing Jules quaking with fear that I'm losing. I'm losing it all.

I pull back to smash my fist against his jaw again. To hear the satisfying crack, but two arms wrap around my chest and pull my back into a hard wall of muscle.

"It's just me. Just calm down," someone says from behind me. An angry growl rumbles through my chest as I throw my head back to smash the fucker's nose in. He leans away and I buck him off of me, ready to beat the piss out of him too.

Until I see who it is. It's Evan, and I can hear Kat scream-ing at him to break us up. They need to stay out of it.

"He tried to hurt her! He put his fucking hands on her!" All the boiling rage rises to the surface and I take it out on Evan. Everyone needs to stay the fuck away.

Liam deserves everything that's coming to him.

I get one more punch in when Liam lurches for me, and his head snaps back from the blow. It lands square on his chin, and my knuckles scream from the sharp impact against his jaw. His lip splits, but it throws him off. As I lunge for-ward, Evan's hand grabs my fist and he twists his body to the side, making me fall forward. He pins my arm behind my back and again grabs me, my back to his chest.

My breath comes in heavy pants and I struggle harder when I hear Jules cry out. I can't see her, and I can't see Liam. I shove backward, but Evan's a strong bastard.

"Knock it off," I hear him grit through his teeth as the sound of a car pulling up catches my attention. I lift my eyes and see the headlights, but no one gets out. No sirens. It's not the cops… yet.

"Think about Jules," he tells me, his breath close to the back of my neck as I push back against his grip. "It's only about Jules, all right?" he says as I stop struggling.

I stare down at the ground, at Liam laying in the snow that's speckled with red. He's propped up on an elbow and on his side. In the bright streaks of light from the limo head-lights, the blood shines a bright red against the pure white snow.

Liam spits, and another splash of red paints the ground.

"Mason," Jules calls out as she runs over to me, and the second my attention goes to her, Evan releases me.

My muscles are still wound tight and ready to go off. My fists still clenched even as she runs into my chest. I kiss her hair as I hear the limo door open and far too many people— too many witnesses—gather around.

"Leave," Evan tells me in a low voice. "It's mine, I'll take yours." He nods behind me and I glance at the white stretch limo before nodding my head. The rough stubble on my chin brushes against Jules's hair. I meet his crystal blue eyes as he says through clenched teeth, "Go! Just get the fuck out of here."

eighteen

Julia

Intentions—cruel, helpless, hopeful,
They come in different shades.
They leave the nights with bright light,
And sharpen the dullest blades.

They bend your will and change your plans,
And make you do bad things.
They don't change the outcome,
Nor stop what justice brings.

MY THUMBNAIL NERVOUSLY SCRAPES AGAINST my fingernails one at a time. I don't have polish on, although I wish I did so I could pick it off. I've always done this. A nervous habit, I suppose.

My eyes drift back to Mason. His head is back against the headrest and it jostles as the limo drives over a speed bump. His hands are clasped in his lap, the knuckles torn and bloodied and his eyes are focused on the roof of the cabin.

His cheek is already bruised. There's a split on the left side of his lips. My fingers itch to touch it. To comfort him.

He hasn't said a word. Silence is the only thing that accompanies us.

I swallow thickly as his head turns to the side and he stares at me. A burning sensation prickles over my skin and begs me to look away, but I can't. It's hopeless.

He licks his lower lip, the tip of his tongue sliding down the cut as he sets his hand on my thigh. I watch as he swallows and then breathes in heavily, all the while holding my gaze. Even blind eyes could see he is a damaged man.

"Are you okay?" he asks in a low voice, deep and heavy and riddled with pain.

"Are you?" I question back with just as much sincerity, but Mason presses on.

"I mean after Liam grabbed you?"

The lump in my throat expands as the memory comes flooding back.

I shake my head immediately, closing my eyes only to recall the unhinged look in Liam's eyes. I shudder and wrap my arms around myself. Mason immediately pulls me into him, holding me. He never fails to comfort me. I breathe easier enveloped in his warmth and resting my head on his chest. I love that he comforts me but just this once, I want to be the one comforting him.

He rocks me softly back and forth for a moment. As I calm down, the guilt weighs heavily on me. Both times now that I've tried to leave Mason, I've come to face regret and remorse for my actions.

"I shouldn't have gone outside," I say, letting the confession drift between us.

"Why were you out there?" Mason asks me, and it only solidifies the offense. I don't answer. Instead I look away, my cheek still resting on his shoulder and his arms still around me.

I hear him swallow and let out a strangled breath before rocking me again ever so slightly. He doesn't let go of me though, and he doesn't question me again. I'm grateful for both.

"I'm sorry," I whisper as I watch the lights of the city slip past us in a blur on our way back to his home.

His deep voice rumbles, "Are you?" There's no animosity there, no curiosity either. Simply a flat question devoid of all the emotion he just gave me a moment ago.

"I am."

A moment passes in silence and the limo rocks us as it passes over another speed bump before Mason kisses my hair and moves me to settle in his lap.

"It's okay," Mason says, running his hand down my hair to my back as he consoles me. He plants a soft kiss on my shoulder and my neck, and then a sweet kiss on my lips before looking me in the eyes. He gives me a sad smile and then kisses me once more before saying, "It's okay, I understand."

His forgiveness is what shatters me. His love and devotion to my happiness are what will ruin me entirely.

"Are you okay?" I ask him genuinely once again, desperate to put the attention and comfort on him. I'll never forget the look in his eyes when he left me. The primal man he became. The way he fought Liam… because of me. My voice catches in my throat as I finally lean toward him and let the tips of my fingers trail over the faint bruise. "I'm sorry," I whisper.

He turns his head, capturing my fingers with his hand and kissing their tips before looking at me. "You have nothing to be sorry for, Jules." His eyes brim with sincerity. "You never did," he says.

Tears prick my eyes, and I don't know which cause is in the forefront. The fear of what happened tonight? The desire to run away from what my life has become?

Or the love I feel for this man.

Maybe it's something instinctual for a woman to want to stay with someone who would fight to protect them. Maybe I feel I owe him for what he's done. All I know is that I can't deny what I feel.

His cold gray eyes stare deep into my own as he cups my chin in his hand and his gaze falls to my lips. He says softly, "I need you, Jules. Even if it's not real…" his voice chokes at the word but he continues with a pained look in his eyes, "Right now, I just need to feel like you love me again."

His hand slips behind my head, holding me still as his fingers tangle in my locks and his hot lips press against mine. I mold my lips to his and part them when he traces the seam with his tongue. My body obeys his and he takes full advantage, pushing against me until my back hits the seat and he settles his hips between my legs. He pins my hips down as he rocks against me, all the while stealing kisses and deepening the intensity. I break away to breathe.

My chest rises as he nibbles along my neck, desire shooting through me and making my nipples pebble.

"I love you, Jules," he whispers into the crook of my neck.

My heart aches. I want to love this man, not because of him, not because of his actions, but because of how I feel about him. A true love-hate relationship. Hot and cold.

I can see myself falling into his arms while simultaneously making plans to sneak out of his bed late at night. I'm ruined beyond repair, and I only blame myself.

nineteen

Mason

It slips through my fingers,
That which I cannot hold.
I cry for it, would die for it,
This love I can't control.

THE ONLY FRIEND I EVER HAD IS DEAD TO ME. The woman I love tried again to leave me, and only came back because she was threatened.

My father may be trying to kill the woman I love. If not him, then someone else.

I've run my business into the ground and with my reputation in the shitter, I don't think I'll ever come back from it.

Last, a secret is out there that could destroy me, evidence that I murdered a man, and I haven't a clue who it is that knows or what they have on me. I'm waiting in the dark, and I can feel my sanity slipping away.

I imagine this is what they mean when they say rock bottom. I slip the heavy law textbook back into its place on the bookshelf as I hear my father's office door open and then close. I don't turn around to face him. I don't have to in order to know it's him.

My father's voice bellows from behind me. "You need to relax, Mason. That shit you pulled—"

"What does it matter?" I say, cutting him off and turning to face him as his forehead creases with anger.

"You look like you've lost it," he hisses at me, slapping the newspaper in his hand down onto his desk as he takes his seat.

"I have though, haven't I?" It's the conclusion I come to, knowing Jules was going to leave me. Again. That's what did me in this time. I take in a heavy breath.

It's all the lies too. Keeping track of them has pulled its weight in bringing me down.

I don't even know what's the truth anymore or who to trust. I only know that I hate everyone I'm surrounded by except for the one person who's desperate to leave me.

"I need the truth," I say, getting straight to the point as I stare my father in the eyes. Although I know it doesn't matter, I add, "Don't lie to me."

"I wouldn't lie to you, Ma—" my father starts, intent on saying something else, but I cut him off.

"You lie to everyone; why would I be any different?" I shrug my shoulders and stride closer to his desk, my pace quick and careless.

"What's on your mind then?" he asks, his eyes narrowed and his frustration barely contained. He must see how on edge I am. I can practically smell the fear coming off of him. The fear of not knowing what I'm going to ask, or maybe of what I'm going to do. "You called this meeting," he adds as he sits back in his cognac leather chair. He unbuttons his suit jacket and adopts a casual posture.

"Did you kill her?" I ask him in a whisper.

He cocks a brow at me before answering in a deathly low voice, "I've never killed anyone."

I don't know why his answer makes my lips tip up into a smile. It's sickening that he doesn't take responsibility. I nod my head, and a rough laugh spills from my lips. "I do apologize," I say as I pace in front of his desk, letting my fingers run over the edges of the leather chair opposite his and then the next. "You *had* her killed."

"You'll have to be more specific as to whom you're referring," my father says as he flicks a switch.

"You think I'm wearing a wire?" I ask incredulously. As if the police could help. As if I wouldn't be completely ruined if I turned to them.

"I don't know what to think about you right now."

I stop in my tracks and face him, bracing a hand on each chair. "I don't either," I say barely above a murmur.

"You were saying?" he says before his eyes shift to the door. This time I know why the smile comes. It's because he wants to get rid of me. He's done with me. It's about fucking time.

"You killed my mother," I say, getting the accusation out into the open once and for all.

"I didn't. I can't believe you'd think that." I stare at him, hearing how false his words sound as they ring in my ears. "There's a difference between killing your own and protecting your own." My father's voice turns hard and at first I think he's justifying having her murdered, but then I realize he's talking about Avery. "Your mother hurt me," he says and leans forward, placing his hand against his chest as he adds, "but I loved her. I would have never done that to her. Or to you."

"I don't believe you," I tell him. "I think you murdered her, and I think you want Jules dead too."

"You have her under control, don't you?" my father says although he knows damn well I don't. After last night, the whole city is talking and now Liam is the topic of the day, not her or me. But three people know what really happened last night.

Jules. Myself. And my father. He knows she wants to leave me. He just doesn't know why.

He doesn't wait for an answer, instead he pulls out a desk drawer and reaches in, rifling through paperwork while he talks. "I looked into Liam's books and subsequent finances." A thick stack of papers lands on his desk with a thud and then he slams the drawer closed. "Would you sit down, Mason? You're going to kill me with this," he says and waves his hands in the air. "Just calm down."

"Calm down?" I ask him before swallowing down the pain, pinching the bridge of my nose as I close my eyes. I've never felt quite like this. Only because the harsh reality has never been so clear to me.

"Mason," my father says my name as if it's a plea, "I promise you, I will protect you with everything I have. If that includes protecting her, I will. You're my son. My one and only, and the only thing I have to live for anymore.

"Whatever it is that's gotten into you," my father continues as he breaks eye contact and shakes his head. "I said I'm sorry about Avery," he adds and presses his lips into a thin line. "You weren't here when she came in." He turns in his chair and looks out of the window. "Or Anderson." He runs a hand down his face and stares out at the city skyline.

"There are choices we make that have to be done quickly." He swallows thickly. "I was only trying to protect you."

I finally take the seat opposite him slowly and wait for him to face me. "No. Stop protecting me." I shake my head slowly and hold his gaze. "I don't want your idea of protection."

"Well maybe this will help," he says as he slides the papers over to me. "Liam Olsen is in the hole, and his life is falling apart."

I hesitantly look through the stack, lifting the corner of the top sheet to look at the next and the one after that. They're all copies of bill after bill he's racked up over the last year.

"We need to talk about what happened the other night before the gala."

It takes me a moment before I realize he's talking about the man with the gun. The intruder with a syringe. An obvious fucking hit. "Someone was hired to kill Jules. I don't know who or why, but it was a hit."

"Are you sure?" my father asks me.

"He could have killed me, he could have turned when I was chasing him and shot me. But then again he could have killed Jules too."

"Then why didn't he?"

I remember the syringe, the heroin. I shift in my seat, staring at my father as I tell him, "He had a syringe on him. He didn't want the hit to be obvious."

My father's expression doesn't change; he doesn't give anything away. "A syringe?"

"Filled with heroin," I tell him and this time he breaks eye contact. He pulls his jacket down and clears his throat, obviously uncomfortable.

"Your mother," he starts to say but doesn't finish. I give him a moment, again remembering the way my mother lay there on the tiled bathroom floor. "So, this is where that shit is coming from?" His question is laced with feigned anger. More than anything, it's a veil over his sadness.

I nod once, not trusting myself to respond verbally.

He nods, although he doesn't look me in the eyes. "Your mother..." he starts to say again and then stops. He waves the thought away, shaking his head and dropping the discussion entirely. I've never seen my father so visibly shaken.

"I don't see why anyone would want you or Jules dead other than Olsen. Even then, it would have to be because of money and I've made it clear to him that the debt owed to me is void. So killing you would most likely be related to some sort of quarrel between the two of you." He finally looks me in the eyes again before adding, "After last night, there must be something between you two... Undoubtedly."

I don't know what possessed Liam to go after Jules last night. I didn't take him for that kind of a man. An arrogant ass, yes. A man who'd hurt a woman? I huff at the thought. Any man who would do something like that isn't a man.

"If not Olsen, who else?"

Every hair stands on end and a chill flows down my

skin. I question telling my father about Anderson, the entire truth. I have no one else, my back's against a wall, and this is for Jules. I would do anything for Jules. If that means confessing murder to a murderer, so be it.

I look my father in the eye as I tell him, "I killed Jace Anderson and someone knows."

I wait for a reaction and the only one I get is that his brows raise slightly and he tilts his head to the side, considering.

"I see," he says after a moment and again turns away from his seat. His foot taps against the desk as he thinks. "Over Avery, I assume?" he says.

I nod once. He has the dignity to look ashamed for a split second.

"You didn't love her. You didn't want her. You told me that much."

"That doesn't make it right," I say and grip the armrests, feeling the anger rise, but he holds up his hands in both defense and understanding.

It's quiet for a moment, with only the ticking of the clock counting the seconds to keep us company as my father takes in the truth of what happened.

Finally, he looks up and says, "You could have come to me."

"I was angry at you too," I say and his eyes spark with indignation at my admission.

As if just now putting the pieces together, his expression changes and he asks, "That's why Jules went to the police? She knows?"

"Yes." I swallow the spiked lump in my throat.

"Who is it who knows?" he asks me, thankfully leaving

the difficulties with Jules out of the conversation. "And what exactly do they know?"

"I don't know," I say and he clicks his tongue against the roof of his mouth. "Jules received an anonymous letter." The paper lays in my wallet as we speak, but I don't present it to him. "It was a warning to get away from me with no evidence."

"Someone knows you killed Jace, warned her to get away from you… but then tried to kill her?" he asks me with confusion.

I nod my head, fully comprehending the lack of logic.

"I don't think they were planning on doing anything when it came to Anderson. They only told Jules to get back at me. And then tried to kill her to keep the secret silenced."

"Who would do that?" he asks me.

You, I think, but I don't say it. I don't have to, though.

His face contorts with disbelief before he turns completely in his chair and opens a cabinet door. I watch in the reflection of the glass, clearly seeing a safe and what's more, the numbers of the combination to open it.

It's the same combination he had on the garage when I was a child. I rip my eyes away from the reflection when he peers back up, holding a stack of photographs in his hand and shutting the door to the safe and then the cabinet with a kick of his foot.

"I wasn't sure if I should show you this or not," he says and lets out an uneasy breath. "It would have complicated things between you and Liam."

I glance down at the photographs and then immediately back up to my father's gaze. *Jace Anderson and Liam's wife, Cecile?*

"No," I say and the word leaves me without my consent.

"They're getting a divorce, so I imagine Liam found out about the affair somehow," my father says absently.

"Maybe Liam? Maybe his wife?" my father says, shrugging. "Either way, I'm sure now that the hit failed, I doubt they'll attempt it again."

His last statement catches me by surprise, and I tear my eyes away from the evidence of Cecile's affair to gauge my father's reaction.

"I'm keeping my ear to the ground and waiting to hear back from a certain someone," he says then shakes his head slightly, "but no one knows anything according to my source."

I can't imagine how deep my father's depravity goes that he has contacts in such low places.

My father continues without looking at me. "I talked to the commissioner." I've been waiting for this. I know there are consequences to what happened the other night. Liam's gunning for me.

"You may have to go in for questioning. You won't be charged with anything, of course. But they have to make it seem like they've done their due diligence." *Thatchers belong on only one side of the courtroom.* It's a saying the men in my family have carried for years.

"I need to go," my father tells me, rising from his seat and gesturing to the door. "If you need help this time, let me know."

CHAPTER

twenty

Julia

It's not the anger toward him,
It's not the dimming fire.
It's not the love I feel for him,
Or how my heart bleeds with desire.
My soul is broken, torn and bent,
Never to repair.
To truly hate oneself,
The sin leaves me in despair.

SEVENTEEN DAYS HAVE PASSED SINCE I GOT THE anonymous letter in the mail.

Each day, Mason looks at me differently. It's like

he knows I'm leaving. I'm not convinced leaving is the answer; I'm not convinced I should stay though either.

The bedroom door creaks open as I brush my hair, getting ready for bed. There's no doubt in my mind that he'll be sleeping in bed with me tonight. He walks into the room quietly, shutting the door behind him. The left side of his face is bruised and cut, but somehow it only adds to his beauty. A prince, wounded in battle saving his princess.

I almost laugh. A hint of it must have escaped at the thought, because he turns to look at me as the door clicks shut. The only light in the room is from the small lamp on the nightstand and the way the shadows sharpen his features does the worst things to me.

There's an odd dynamic between the two of us. He wants to touch me, he keeps coming close to doing just that, circling me and waiting, but he doesn't.

The part that's truly insane is that it disappoints me, every single time. I'm crazy for feeling any attraction to him at all, but I'm drawn like a moth to a flame.

He picked me up when I fell.

He protected me when I was weak.

And even though I hate him for what he's done, he's the only reason I'm still alive.

"You can't hide in here forever, Jules," Mason comments half-heartedly with a small smile on his lips that doesn't reach his eyes. He closes the space between us easily, and I let him. His lips brush against mine in what I presume will be a gentle kiss, but he deepens it and without my conscious consent, I lean into it. I didn't realize how much I missed his touch.

He moans into my mouth as he kisses me deeply, not

holding back a damn thing. I wish I could do the same, but all I find myself doing is forcing myself to stay away, to keep my guard up around him. I can't let myself fall again. I won't. I utterly refuse to give him that chance or else I know he'll keep me forever. And I don't know who exactly I'll be if I let that happen.

I break the kiss before he's finished with me, but he only pushes harder into me, wanting more and letting me know exactly what he needs.

I turn away from him, shame filling every piece of me. Ashamed to be kissing him. Ashamed that I *want* to kiss him.

"Is that how you want it, Jules?" he asks and his deep voice comes out rough as I look into his eyes. The passion is still there. The desire that ignites mine stares back at me.

"You want to hate me." He brings his lips to my ear, making a burning ache flow down every inch of my skin. "Try hating me while you cum on my dick, sweetheart," he tells me and I know I'm done for. My head falls back, hitting the wall as his hands trail over my sides, slowly making their way down my curves.

He rakes his teeth down my collarbone, the sensation directly linked to both my sensitive nipples and needy clit. I'm desperate for more. Aching for him to take me and own my body like I know only he can. His teeth sink into the crook of my neck as his hands pin my hips down, holding me in place as I cry out in sheer frustration.

His large body towers over me, the heat from his body suffocating me as his hard erection digs into my lower belly.

"Fight me, Jules," he says, gripping the hair at the nape of my neck and twisting it around his wrist. "Fight me like you want to."

I slap him, his rough stubble scraping against my hand. A low growl rumbles up his chest; it's just as filthy and perverted as I feel, keenly aware of how much he turns me on. I press both of my hands against his chest, a weak and helpless attempt at pushing him away and he just chuckles at me, his gray eyes flickering to life with a heat I've missed. Nothing but wanting moans escape my lips.

He grabs the nape of my neck, forcing my head to tilt and claiming a cry from me as he steals a kiss along my jaw. I shove my weight forward, attempting to push him away with more vigor, but he merely uses my attempt to push and twist me down onto the bed.

My belly presses against the mattress, my back arching as he stands behind me, leaning against me and pinning me down as his fingertips slide up my outer thighs.

My heart squeezes too tightly without being able to see him and feel him. I don't know why, but I don't want this, not like this.

"Mason," I call out for him, and his name is nothing more than a plea with the frantic need I feel.

He instantly braces his forearms around me, no longer touching me and no longer pinning me to the bed. He breathes heavily, panting as I turn slowly, still caged under him. It's an awkward way to lie, with my bottom barely on the edge of the bed.

His eyes are closed, shut tight and his plump lips parted as I lie beneath him. A caged animal, hurt and tortured and needing a way out is all I see. "Mason," I whisper his name and he opens his eyes.

I gently press my lips to his, taking a sweet kiss before nipping his bottom lip. I brush the tip of my nose against his, and the spark ignites again. He attempts a soft kiss, but it quickly turns into something else. Something primal and filled with lust.

He kisses down my neck, over the small bite marks still red on my skin and aching for attention. He strips my underwear from me and kicks off his own as we slowly climb deeper into the bed. Slowly parting from our clothes and the worries that wait beyond the heavy sheets.

I don't stop whispering his name, I don't stop pushing and pulling against him until he slams into me, filling me and stretching my walls in one swift thrust. My back arches, and a silent scream rips up my throat.

The pleasure he gives me is unmatched, indescribable and something only for us. It's sinful and wrong, but it feels like heaven.

A strangled moan is torn from me and he almost stops when I push against his cheek yet again. I can see the hesitation, the worry in his eyes. I arch my neck and rock my hips, letting him know that I'm his. That I want this and him just the same. My head thrashes from side to side as my throbbing clit brushes against his rough pubic hair as he stills deep inside of me, buried to the hilt and hovering over me, watching my expression. "More," I whimper, desperate for whatever he will give me. I'm deprived without his touch. He should know that; he's done this to me.

Crashing his lips against mine, he moves his hand to my hip, positioning me how he wants me and tilting my ass up just slightly so he can thrust deeper into me. He slams himself harder and deeper into me, unrelenting and unmerciful. "Fuck," I moan, and he's quick to echo my pleasure.

From him, it's a groan of awe filled with gratitude and

devotion, fueling him to push me farther and farther as he races for his release. He whispers the word over and over in the crook of my neck, his hot breath sending chills over my body.

From me, it's a strangled cry as my nails scratch down his back and my body pleads for more and also to run from the intensity. It's a mix of pleasure and pain, a cocktail strong enough to kill me and I don't know which one it will be that finally brings me to my death.

twenty-one

Mason

ITS DIFFICULT TO CONFRONT A PERSON WHEN THEY have a restraining order against you. Regardless, I consider driving by Liam's house, knocking on the door and beating the fucking piss out of him all over again. A week has passed, and not a damn thing has changed. The air is stagnant and I don't know what to do but I won't sit and wait for the next onslaught.

The once sought-after developer and bachelor has taken a fall.

The excerpt of the news article lays above my mug shot.

At least I knew it was coming; the journalist was decent enough to give me a heads-up. Evan could only do so much to hold me back from Liam, but he worked as much magic as he could with the press.

It's only a mug shot. No charges pressed and nothing on my record, but the city has a way of talking. The most shocking thing in the article is the information concerning Liam. Apparently he has a criminal record from college for assault and battery, and attempts at much worse. Divorce papers have already been signed between him and his now ex-wife, and the article compares that to the supposed breakup between Jules and myself.

I'm not sure what is true concerning Liam. I'm grateful the spotlight is on him in the article. The article got my father and Jules all worked up. I can only imagine how they'd react if they knew about the letter that arrived today too.

The paper in my hands rustles in the quiet office as I read it again.

I was mad at you for what you did, and I'm sorry.
It's not what you think.
The gentleman was only there to find something, but I found it elsewhere.

I'm sorry for what I've done.
And I forgive you for what you did; I hope you can forgive me as well.

Sincerely,
X

It's the same feminine writing as the other note. This one sits in my wallet, and it's been here for hours, refusing to allow me to think of anything else.

Whoever it was is damn good at concealing their identity. Not a single fingerprint on the envelope or the paper itself. The security footage shows it was delivered by the mailman, but has no return address. I'm lost, and I have absolutely no leads.

I finally crumple the letter, hating it and the fucker more now than ever. The hopeless feeling weighs down on me. I can't fix it. I can't fix anything without knowing who to blame.

They fucked with me, ruined something so precious and perfect, tearing Jules from my life. And now they're just backing away? They wanted to destroy me. Mission fucking accomplished.

I don't know who to trust anymore or what to live for. My only hope is to pretend it's all right. To move through life like nothing's wrong, and pray that Jules can one day do the same. The rough edges of the letter rub harshly against my skin as I close my eyes and tighten my fist around it. It's never going to happen.

She's never going to forgive me.

She loves me deep down. She has to. I can't feel this strongly about her without her feeling something for me.

Tossing the letter into the small trash can beneath my desk, I rise from my seat and wonder about my father, about Liam's wife and how she plays into this. But this game is so much different than any other I've played before.

Too many pieces and moving parts, but I can't see a damn one of them.

It feels a lot like giving up. A lot like losing. But

sometimes you need to keep going through the motions, stay on your guard, and just let them think you've lost.

I flick off the light switch as I open the office door and stand there in the hall, contemplating where Jules is most likely to be in the house. My hand tightens on the doorknob, as I wonder if she'll talk to me like we used to. If she'll let me hold her. If those moments when she forgets and looks at me with those gorgeous blue eyes will last longer than seconds tonight.

I'll leave it be, if only to let them think I've lost and given up. I nod my head as I leave; that's what I tell myself.

As I shut the door behind me, it feels like I truly have lost everything already.

CHAPTER
twenty-two

Julia

I**T'S NEARLY PICTURE PERFECT.**

To anyone looking in, we're a couple sitting on the sofa in front of a roaring fire.

There's plenty of lighting for the scene in Mason's living room. The light's brighter and has been all winter with the curtains open and the snow covering the grounds. The white reflects the sunshine into the room, no matter how dim it is. I watch the flames lick along the log. This fireplace is different from the one in the dining room. It's odd they don't match. I would've changed that if it were up to me. But it wasn't. Because this isn't where I belong.

I'm trapped here. I've made up my mind and I'm done.

I swallow thickly, moving more of the blanket over my chest as Mason shifts on the other end of the sofa. I came down here to write and to get this tale out of my head. To put an ending on it and hoping I could get a different perspective, but these words that stare back at me make me want to scream. Scratching out the lines over and over, I attempt to change them and deny it, but it is what it is. There's no changing this ending.

My foot brushes against the pad of paper on the ottoman as I turn to face Mason.

He's working, too, but completely unaffected. If I had to pinpoint what's caused the finality and resentment, it's the way he continues; I hate how easily he can move forward.

I've heard of that psychological condition where the woman falls for her captor. Stockholm syndrome. That's not what this is. I loved this man with my whole heart before. I can feel myself falling, slipping back into that place and I refuse to go there.

He brought me into this hell, and I want out. I need to get out.

I'm scared, and I don't know what to do. But I know I need to be alone. That's what it comes down to. I'm destroyed, and I need to be okay alone.

I'll never stop loving him, but I need to stop hating myself and I can't do that if I'm with him. "This isn't a life," I blurt out and then look up at Mason. "I want to leave, Mason."

He doesn't look at me at first, but he stops typing. The quiet clacking of the keys turns to nothing, leaving the room silent but for the crackling of the fire.

When he turns to look at me, I can see the fight in him

is almost gone. He's almost given up as well. It shouldn't crush me the way it does. It shouldn't cause this pain. This hole in my chest, but it does.

Taking a moment to swallow, the cords in his neck tighten before he answers, "You told me that you'd give me a month."

A sadistic laugh leaves me—one that's terrifying and rude, one that I should feel apologetic for letting slip out, but I can't keep up with all the lies like he does. "You and I both know it's never going to happen." The words come out like a knife—knives, really. They cut us both, each in different ways.

"You can't leave," he tells me simply and I can't help but feel enraged.

"I'm not staying," I state with finality and narrow my eyes at him, and I feel a side of me that wants to fight. Not like the other night. I want to fight for my life. For my freedom and for a happiness I don't ever see myself having with Mason. Not ever again.

"There's someone—"

"I don't care," I spit at him. "I can take care of myself."

His voice holds a note of admonishment as he says, "Don't be stupid, Jules."

"Fuck you," I hiss, gripping the sofa as I lean closer to him. "I was fine before I met you." I'm on edge, and violence brews inside of me. "How dare you!" I yell at him. I hold on to the anger. It's the only sane part of me anymore. "How dare you start this when you knew from the very beginning—" My voice gets so tight I can't finish.

Mason stares at me, judging how to handle me. It's what he does, but this is too much for either of us. High and mighty with his tone, he pushes back, "You were lonely, and don't pretend—"

"Because of you!" I scream the interruption, my voice and throat raw and full of pain. "You did this to me!" I yell. "I'm not okay, and it's because I'm fucking you!" All of my pent-up rage, all the boiling anger spills over and I kick out, throwing the blanket off and getting away from him. There's not enough distance between us, only feet from where he sits and where I stand. I can't leave though, not until he lets me go. Our stares are locked, brutalized with both sadness and anger.

It's quiet for a moment, with only the sounds of my heavy breathing and the fire.

"You need me to fix it," Mason says with confidence.

"You can't fix this," I say dully and my heart hurts as I answer him. I wish he could. I so desperately wish he could fix this. Because I want him. I want to love him, and have him forever. But that isn't our ending. I swallow and say, "You can't fix this."

"You need me—"

"I don't need anyone." I cut him off, letting out a deep breath and slowly lifting my head to look him in the eyes. The silver specks pierce through me as I say, "Mason, I'm done with all this. I'm done." The last two words of my confession are only whispers.

His expression softens as he leans back and I take the seat on the far end of the sofa, wanting the tension to leave us both. "Do you hate me?" he asks, his eyes turning glossy but I know he won't cry. That's not the man Mason is. I already know he loves me. I know he wants me. I know I want him too, but that's not in our cards. He decided that long ago, before he even met me.

"No." My voice croaks as I answer him and that hurts so much worse, telling him and confessing. "I don't hate you, it's not you."

He huffs a sarcastic and defensive sound. "It's not you, it's me," he says as he slams his laptop shut and pushes it off of him.

I lick my dry lips, feeling the cracks with the tip of my tongue. "You know it's what you've done, Mason." I wait for him to look at me again and I sniffle, wiping my tears and nose with my sleeve. "It's who you used to be that I can't get over.

"It's not about you, or what you want. It's about me being okay with this, and I never will be. How can I?" I shrug, wiping the tears as they come carelessly.

"Let me hold you," Mason says although it sounds like a demand, reaching out for me, but I move away, taking the throw with me in haste and then letting it fall to the floor.

"I can't," I say with my back to him. I tell him, "If you touch me, I don't think I'll be able to go."

"Then don't," he says with desperation, but he doesn't move.

"I can't forget, I can't pretend. And I hate myself for loving you." It's the hate I can't live with. I turn to face him, pleading with him to understand and accept it. "I hate myself."

I watch as Mason stands and leaves, as the first tear rolls down his cheek and he brushes it away angrily.

I can't let him walk away like this. I reach out to him, gripping onto his arm and he stops but doesn't look at me.

"Mason, please," I say, begging him, but I don't know what for. "I don't want to hurt you."

He shakes his head as he tells me, "It's my fault." That's all he says as I stand there waiting for more. My body wars with me, wanting to cave and let him hold me. I haven't realized it until now, but all this time, holding me has been his only way to be held in return.

"I need to give you your gun," Mason says in a tight voice, looking past me and toward the stairs.

"You're giving me the gun?" I ask him more as a distraction from standing there so numb and full of despair than anything else.

He nods once.

"And you'll leave me alone?" I ask him, both wanting him to tell me yes and give in to my wishes, and also to tell me no and say he'll love me forever.

"Yes," he says and my heart breaks into two. "I'll watch over you," he says as he nods his head and I nod in return, reflexively. "When you're safe," he says and swallows thickly before continuing, "I'll leave you alone. I promise."

twenty-three

Mason

Time be still,
Show me a way.
To turn back what's done,
And change our yesterday.
I'm so damn sorry,
I would repent,
Alas, that time is already spent.

THERE'S NO WAY I'M LEAVING HER ALONE.

In time, she'll forgive me. I'm sure she will. It's easier to ask for forgiveness, isn't it? That's how the saying goes.

A heavy sigh leaves me as I climb back into my car and double-check every window of her place. I've got a security system in place so she can be alone during the day, but at night, I'm slipping in through the back like I used to. I'll be quiet. I won't let anyone see. Not even her if she doesn't want to.

It wouldn't be right to leave her alone, but I can still let her leave.

The leather behind me protests as I close my eyes, leaning my head back with an overwhelmingly pathetic feeling consuming me. Everything I've done is to protect her, yes. But I can't let her go. I'm holding on to the last bit of her that I can. She's slipping, running away from me and I'd be a liar to say it doesn't shred me.

It's been weeks of nothing. Weeks of waiting. I don't believe for a moment whoever wrote that note and sent that man is done with me. Or with her.

I press the button on my phone for the security feed. I have it all here. I'll keep her safe.

I'll know the second anyone enters. The locks are all new. The alarms are set. Every door that opens in that house, I'll be alerted—same with every window.

She doesn't want to stay with me, and I can't force her to love me enough to stay. But I'll protect her and care for her. I have nothing and no one else. I have no choice.

The keys jingle as I start my car and the heater blows out cold air while the radio plays soft music. I turn them both off and listen to the hum of the engine. Taking another look over my shoulder and then another glance at the feed on my phone, I make a promise to let her go one day, just not today. I'll leave her alone like she wants. I'll let her move on and live a normal life.

I can never give her that, I know that. Not with the way our worlds collided. She deserves that with someone else.

My throat feels tight as I gently press the pedal down and pull away from her row of condos on the Upper East Side. There's still a chance if I just hold on… I won't have to let her go. She'll forgive me.

My warring thoughts storm through me. Let her go or hold on to hope.

Even knowing how wrong it is, I'll be back tonight. I can't leave her alone. I can't let her go. That truth always wins out.

twenty-four

Julia

When did life become like this?
When did I lose it all?
When did my will to move on,
Become my wish to fall?
When was it that I gave up?
I'm a hollow, empty shell.
There's no answer that I know of,
And no way out of this hell.

EVERYWHERE I LOOK, I SEE MY DEAD HUSBAND. Lying in bed, sitting on a chair. He haunts this house in a way he never has before. It's not fear I'm feeling when the ghost of him appears as distant memories. It's anger.

I shouldn't have come back here.

I ran away from a man I love, only to come back to a past I hate.

My reflection is pale in the mirror. The bags under my eyes are back, and I look like shit. I wipe the fog from the shiny surface. The steam of the shower still lingers. It's late and I'm drained, both physically and emotionally, but I can't sleep.

Not without Mason next to me. I'm cold without him and feel weaker than I do when I'm with him. Maybe that's the way I trained myself. To be brave when there's someone to lean on. *What kind of bravery is that?*

I swallow the lump in my throat and close my eyes. I tell myself that I was wrong to love him, and somehow fooled into thinking it was real. If I convince myself it was never real, it will be so much easier to let go.

Opening my eyes only reveals the men of my past surrounding me in the mirror. Mason on my right, and Jace on my left, standing next to me in the reflection.

I blink once, and they're gone.

Leaving me alone, and isn't that what I wanted?

A chill runs through my blood as I focus on just breathing and calming myself. Bottles of perfume are lined up so neatly on the shelf. Chanel Chance is the first one in the row of expensive and elegant bottles. My breathing comes in harsh pants as I stare at it. It's nearly halfway empty. It was a Christmas gift.

I wonder if he gave his mistresses the same kind of gifts? What about the woman he had killed? *The one pregnant with his child?*

The last thought snaps my last bit of control. A wretched cry echoes in the bathroom, burning my throat as I whip my hand across the shelf. The tinkling, crashing and shattering of glass fills the room as I stand there heaving. I grip the edge of the bathroom door, tears blurring my vision and stare back at myself. I fucking hate who I was. Naïve and stupid. "So fucking stupid!" I scream at myself. "I hate you!" I yell out. "I hate what you did to me!"

My body sways as I harshly wipe under my eyes, turning from the mirror before I shatter it as well. The overwhelming scent of the perfumes mix in the air and I slam the door shut behind me, hating how it reeks and how the mess from my outburst, reckless and yet again stupid, will stay there until I clean it up. I'll be the one picking up the tiny pieces of shattered glass. That's how it works when these men storm in, destroying everything and demanding I follow their lead.

Jace's closet is across from the bathroom. It was untouchable before when he passed. I couldn't bear to open it and see all of his clothes. Suits he would never wear again. Shirts that held memories.

I rip the doors open chaotically, but then pause and walk in ever so slowly, flicking on the light. The U-shaped closet is lined with crisp white dress shirts and a myriad of colors on the left. Suits on the right. In the very back is his collection of soccer jerseys. He started buying them all the way back in high school. I remember the first one he ever got. I spot it as the memory comes flooding back.

I told him the red brought out his eyes.

I clench my teeth as I tear the shirt down. The fabric feels like nothing in my fisted hand.

I told him how handsome he looked in it.

A scream I don't recognize as my own joins me when I grab the others, tearing them off the hangers and tossing them onto the floor.

He whispered that he wanted to see me in nothing but the jersey.

I kick the pile of jerseys aside and then dump the suits onto the floor, screaming as the memory washes over me.

I smiled, I wore it just for him and made love to him for the first time in that fucking jersey.

"I hate you!"

I blushed with innocence and handed everything I had right over to him. "I'll never forgive you!"

I don't stop until every last garment is littered on the floor. I take a shaky breath, not knowing if it's him I hate or myself.

My gaze searches the closet for something, anything to validate my rage. I tear open shoeboxes looking for little black books. Ripping through the drawers of a small watch armoire I tear them all out, flinging the cold metal behind me.

Each is a moment I wish I could take back.

Support that I'd given him blindly. The trust. Our marriage vows that meant nothing to him.

There's nothing that overtly makes him a *bad man* in this closet. No evidence that he deserved to die. There's nothing here. Nothing but ghosts of the past and memories I haven't suffered through in a year.

My shoulders rise and fall heavily as I move from one post to the next, focusing on taking it all down. I can't stand to see his things hanging there.

It's all the memories and the details he hid from me.

They don't deserve their place anymore. I can't stand it and I want them gone.

I know deep in my gut that everything Mason told me is true. I always go with my gut, and it led me here. Crying in the middle of a trashed closet, with my prick of a dead husband's clothes scattered around me.

I'm searching for anything. Anything at all that would tell me it's okay to hate Jace and be done with him forever. That everything Mason said is true, and therefore it's okay to love him. That it's okay… for him to have murdered Jace.

I use the sleeve of a suit to bury my face. The cool material makes my heated face feel even hotter. I've finally lost it.

"I'll hate you forever, Jace Anderson." Exhaustion makes my legs shaky and I just want to lie down. I want to wake up and forget it all. I push the hair out of my face, taking in a deep breath.

My eyes close, and I see Mason. His gorgeous smile, and those deep gray eyes full of so much emotion.

I wish I could smile. I wish I could go to him and beg him to take me back. That's how far gone I am. I open my eyes, promising myself to be strong, but I can't walk another step.

My body tingles with awareness and fear as I look straight ahead.

The balcony doors are closed, but unlocked.

I know they were locked. My body feels frozen as I look to my left, the gun still in plain sight on my nightstand.

I look back to the balcony, staring at the lock and knowing without a doubt that someone else is in this house.

twenty-five

Mason

D RESSED IN ALL BLACK, I'M CERTAIN I'LL SLIP into the night for most people as I casually stroll along the sidewalk to William Street Towers, my father's office building. It's late and although the building is unlocked, the offices inside are locked up and most of the lights are off.

Opening the main door, my blood heats with anxiety as it swings open. The cameras are on. I don't have to look up at the little red lights to know they're recording.

My posture is relaxed, and I'll act like I belong. I won't appear out of place in the least. It's silent in the building as I rock on my heels and hit the button for the elevator.

Someone coughs to my right, and I chance a look at a woman in a pencil skirt walking quickly to the narrow hallway where the restrooms are. A lone soul, working late.

This is how men go to prison for life for crimes they committed, but didn't get caught for.

This is how you fuck up and drown in your past mistakes for something so damn stupid.

An arrest for trespassing, or breaking and entering? They could charge me with that, and it wouldn't be the worst thing to have happened to me.

But they won't stop there. If I get caught, then my father will find out. He'll know what I was doing. He can push, and the powers that be will sentence me harsher than justice would allow.

This is how men are taken down. For doing stupid shit, rather than keeping their noses clean. But I don't give a damn. I need to know what's in that safe. I need answers.

It's been itching at me, an irritating thought in the back of my head, over and over ever since I left. A nagging that won't stop and a whisper that tells me everything is there, right there.

He had information on Liam… what else does he have in that safe?

The elevator dings as it arrives, the doors parting for me and sealing my fate.

Miss Theresa Geist has a bad habit. I'm not sure if anyone else knows, but growing up so close to her, spending so much time with her, I've learned that she sometimes forgets her keys. She takes the subway to work, and it's happened more than a time or two.

Because of this, she leaves the main office key tucked in the drawer of the reception desk in the hallway. It's hidden in a false bottom to the drawer. Or at least she used to hide it there. I swing the large glass door open and my heart races as I commit the first crime tonight, knowing it's being recorded. Knowing it's capturing my face.

It doesn't matter. It won't matter unless the cops or security have to pull up the tapes for a reason.

I swallow thickly, picking up the tray of paper clips and collection of pens and thumbtacks.

A small smile curves my lips up as I find the key. I stare at it a moment, watching it gleam in the lights from the hallway. It'll only get me into his practice's section of the building, but his office lock can be picked now that I'll be completely out of sight.

Open from 7:00 a.m. to 6:00 p.m. The white letters look back at me as I slip in the key and unlock the door.

With the soft click, all I can think is that I should have done this weeks ago. I prop the door open with a desk chair and return the key to where it belongs. No one will be the wiser. I should have come in here the moment I knew about the safe and the combination to its secrets.

But Jules was still with me.

She was still in my house and in my bed. Still a target if something were to happen to me. Everyone knows she's left me, thanks to the article in the morning paper.

Everyone is very aware that she left me after the incident that occurred at the gala. Or at least that's what's being read in black and white.

My heart clenches and I grit my teeth, kicking the chair back as I head straight for my father's door in the back. I slip my hand into my pocket, feeling the bent paper clips there. My fingers travel up and down the thin metal.

She would never do something like this. Jules isn't capable of it. I smile and a rough laugh slips through my lips as I stop at his door and slide the paper clips into the lock. Back in the day, I was damn good at this.

Jules would hate to know all the shit I did years ago. My pulse slows at the thought, turning cold, beating in time with the lock clicking and then the knob turns. I push open the door slowly, ignoring the memories.

The room is brighter than the hall was. The city lights pour through the blinds, creating alternating stripes of light and shadow throughout the room.

I don't waste any time, letting the door shut behind me and moving to his desk, to the cabinet. It swings open easily as if there's no challenge at all presenting itself.

I hesitate only for a moment, realizing whatever's in the safe may tell me more than I ever wanted to know.

There may be evidence of him murdering my mother. It's the first thought that comes to mind, and inwardly I curse myself. It's been twenty years.

Slipping on leather gloves first, I press the buttons slowly, mimicking my father's movements although the safe itself looks typical and ordinary. My lungs still, and my blood rushes in my ears as I wait for the light to flash and the small click that tells me it's unlocked.

It was far too easy.

Piles of paper lay in the safe. Stacks of photographs are the first that I remove, right where he kept the ones of Liam's wife and Jace Anderson. The photos are still on top. I flip through them, still in disbelief. How the hell did she even know him?

The stack directly underneath the one my father showed

me makes me do a double take. I grab the photo of Jace and Cecile together and hold it next to a photo of Cecile alone. As I compare the two, my anger rises.

I've always known he was a liar.

It's altered. The photo is faked. My shoulders rise and fall with a tense breath.

Why set her up? They're already getting a divorce. *It's for you*, a soft voice whispers in the back of my head. *It was all to convince you it wasn't him. He'd let anyone else take the fall.*

I slip the photo back into place and scan through the others, searching for shots of Jules or myself, or anything else that proves what a conniving bastard my father is.

The next print is of someone I don't know. I'm confused at first because I have no idea why it was even taken. There's nothing remotely scandalous about it. I stare at the man in question and try to place him. It takes me a moment before I realize it's Jules's CPA, her financial advisor. The prick she went to go see months and months ago. I make it a habit to know who she interacts with. Why him? It doesn't make sense. Maybe he blackmailed him into doing something. I'm not sure.

I stop short at the next stack. It's a letter.

I stare at the photograph of Avery's blackmail letter. Her signature is there. I remember how she used to sign her name. Her handwriting was distinct when she signed documents. All I ever saw was her signature. The curves though, the curves of her writing are so familiar.

My blood runs cold. It's not possible.

It's her handwriting in the notes. I turn to the next photograph and it's another letter from Avery. No it's not. It's just a list of what looks like groceries.

I flip to the next, and that's when I realize what these are. Photographs of her handwriting. My skin pricks with an unforgiving chill. I set the photographs down after searching through several more stacks, but not finding anything at all that makes sense.

I lay them on the seat of the leather chair before looking back into the safe.

There's cash stuffed in the bottom. I take a stack of bound hundred-dollar bills and look behind them, shuffling the money to be sure that's all that's at the bottom. There must be over a million here. Although the safe is small, most of it is stacked with nothing but the bundled hundreds. So much money, it reeks of wealth.

I shove it back into place, not giving two shits about it, and that's when my eyes are drawn up to the top shelf. A thin, brown leather-bound notebook leans against the upper compartment of the safe where the photos were. I take it out, wondering what he'd confess in a bound journal, or if it's even his. I expect to find names and dollar amounts. Or names and account numbers, something of that nature. Information that's irrelevant to what I'm after.

The list of addresses I see first, I recognize immediately. They're ones Anderson bought, the ones my company wanted. But next to them are columns of figures. Dollar amounts of what they sold for at the time of purchase, and what they're projected to be worth after the surrounding properties are developed.

My forehead pinches not understanding why he'd give a shit. He doesn't own them, and they aren't for sale. They never were. Next to the dollar amounts are dates. A word has been repeatedly scribbled in tiny cursive next to some of them, but it's hard to make it out. I squint, my lips moving as I try to figure it out.

Acquired.

He bought them. They're investments. He had a plan, and everyone played a role. But Anderson had no intention of selling. He'd made that clear in the single meeting I had with him. Maybe he knew the properties would go up in value. Or maybe he wanted more money.

I run my fingers over the list of numbers as I try to piece together what corrupt business transaction the two men had together, but that's when I come across something familiar. Something I've become intimately acquainted with these past few weeks.

In the back of the notebook, there are several sheets of paper. Paper I'd consider elegant under other circumstances.

But this paper almost made me lose everything.

The thick cream parchment is unmistakable. My hand clenches into a fist as I fall onto my ass. My back hits the cabinet door as I picture my father writing the letters.

Practicing Avery's handwriting. Planning his next move. I was a target, and so was she.

It was him. It was always him. It's that moment when an alert sounds on my phone. *Jules.*

twenty-six

Julia

Emotions will trap you,
You have no choice.
Those bitter words?
That's not your voice.
They play with your mind,
And take over your will.
Anger is deadly, and
Fear can kill.

THE GUN IS HEAVY AND IT SLIPS IN MY HANDS AS I slowly walk down the steps, careful not to make too much noise. I cringe each time the stairs creak. So much noise. My hands are sweaty and my heart races as I move down the stairs with my back against the wall.

Thud, thud, thud, my heartbeat is loud in my ears. Too loud; I can barely hear anything else beyond the constant rhythm.

Barely breathing, my gaze flickers to the front door and then back up the staircase as light creeps in through the stained glass. I hold my breath until my feet land on the cold tile of the foyer. The front door is only feet away but as I get there, footsteps sound from the other side. The knob rattles, and my heart attempts to climb up my throat.

Whoever it is doesn't knock or ring the bell. I wait for a moment, trembling as I grip the gun for dear life, praying they'll prove to be someone I know, but there's only silence on the other side.

My heart is pounding harder now as I quietly race down the hallway, looking ahead and checking behind me every few seconds. *I need to escape out the back.*

The closed-in backyard won't do me any good, but I can climb the fence and slip through the thin veil of a forest straight to the crowded sidewalks of the city.

So close to protection, so close to safety. *Just run.*

I pause, my back pressed firmly against the wall as I get to the edge and peek around the corner and into the living room.

It's empty, and only fifteen or so feet to the sliding doors.

I'll run. The moment the thought occurs, I take off. But a sudden clatter in the kitchen startles me and I scream out, fumbling the gun and falling on my ass. I cover my mouth and turn quickly to face whoever's there. My pulse races and my body trembles.

The gun landed behind me and I struggle to reach it, my arms propping me up. I keep my eyes forward, though. I'm shocked to find I'm staring at Liam Olsen.

"Whoa," he says easily, a smile on his face. "There you are," he says like he's been waiting for me. Like he's been expecting me. He takes two steps forward and my fear intensifies as he bends down, picking up a magnet that was on the fridge.

"It fell," he says with a shrug.

"What are you doing here?" I barely get out the question as I stand slowly, bringing the gun up behind my back and placing my finger next to the trigger.

"I was told you wanted to talk about something very important?" Liam's tone is playful, teasing and with a grin, he starts loosening the tie around his neck. "That you wanted—"

I bring the gun out in front of me slowly and steady my hands.

Liam's hands go up instantly, his eyes wide with shock.

"I don't want to talk about anything," I tell him and my voice shakes. My body is on fire, and the only thing pumping in my blood other than adrenaline is fear. The memories of the other night come back full force. His hands on me, his lips so close to my neck. "Stay away from me!" I scream at him, and the force of my emotions makes me tremble.

"All right now, you need to put that down," he says with more authority than he has, although his expression is still riddled with worry. He takes a step forward, arms still raised.

"I said stay away!" I cry out as if I'm scared and powerless, because that's how I feel. "Get the fuck out!"

"I'm going, I'm going," Liam says quickly. "I came in through the front and I'm headed out the front door, okay?"

He says the words quickly, his own breathing ragged. "There must've been a misunderstanding," he tells me quickly, rushing out the words. Just then, his gaze rises just a touch higher, his focus no longer on me, but instead trained on something behind me. I didn't hear the back door sliding open until it was too late, and my skin pricks with the realization that I'm trapped. *There's someone behind me.*

I scream and as I do, the gun slips again in my sweaty grip and goes off. My eyes dart to it and it's like I'm watching in slow motion as it happens.

The sound of the bang.

The kick of the gun, making my arms jerk.

Large hands settle on my shoulders as the scream tears up my throat.

The bang still resonates in my ears as my body shakes and I try to push the man behind me away, but he holds me close as he says, "It's okay!"

I can hardly breathe, let alone recognize the voice.

Fear is what guided everything. I swear. I didn't mean for any of it to happen.

I look up and into the eyes of Mason, only it's not him. It's his father, looking down at me with sympathy, with sadness and horror.

Only when I see it's him do I look back at Liam.

The blood drains from my body when I see he's not moving. He's face-down, his arm at an awkward angle. "Liam," I call out, but he doesn't answer.

The gun is hot in my hands. A sickness grows in my stomach.

I shake my head over and over. What happened? I didn't. I swear I didn't shoot him.

Mason's father grips me again and I stumble backward, desperate to get away from him. My legs kick out as I scramble across the floor.

"Leave me alone!" I yell at him, still holding the gun, but pointing it toward the ground. *He isn't dead. I didn't kill him. I didn't mean to pull the trigger.*

He lets me go and says with nothing but compassion, "I saw what happened. It was an accident." He almost whispers the words. His eyes are wide as he nods. "It's okay, I saw it."

His words are comforting.

It was an accident. I swear it was. I look back at the body on the floor, my vision blurred from tears. *It was an accident. How did this happen? Why are they here?*

Too many questions scream in my head. Too many things are so very wrong. I look up at him with desperation and say, "Please, help me." My face crumples as the sobs start. "Save him."

What have I done?

twenty-seven

Mason

THE DOOR IS ALREADY OPEN AS I STORM INTO THE house. Everything rages inside of me. I drove as fast as I could. But it's not fast enough. I've never prayed so much in my life as I did on my way to her place.

Bang! I swear I heard a gunshot, and I've never felt so cold in my life. The only thing keeping me from dying inside as I race through the first floor of her place, is hearing her cry. It means she's still alive.

"Jules!" I call out her name just as I get to her living room, all the way in the back of the townhouse.

My world spins as I stop short in the room. My father's hands are on Jules's shoulders, and Liam is dead on the floor.

"It was an accident," she whimpers over and over and Jules's hands shake as the gun falls to the floor.

"It's all right," my father whispers into her ear. "I saw it," he says and looks up at me, "it was an accident." His statement is firm. Just like his grip on her. He nods and I can already see the wheels spinning. He set this up. It's the ending he wrote. Liam the villain, and he gets to be the hero. Liam's wife gets his properties, then my father can buy them. Jules and I have our villain and he's in the clear.

Everything clicks into place. Each event, everything he's done and how he's played each piece.

I take a careful step forward, so aware of how close he is to her and the gun. *Too close.*

"Mason," Jules cries out. God I want to go to her, I desperately want to hold her, but as I take another step closer, my only goal is to get between the two of them. To keep him away from her.

This all ends tonight. I won't let him live to breathe the same air as us. His greed is deadly. If he did it once, he'll do it again.

"Stay behind me," I say as I rip Jules away from my father, grabbing her hand and forcing her behind me. I kick the gun behind me as well as I keep my gaze on him. His cold gray eyes darken and narrow at me.

"You can't pin this on me," he huffs. Naturally he'd think I was trying to save her and destroy him. It's all he's ever thought. Everyone's always out to get him. This time I am.

"Stay away from her." I swallow and say, "It was you."

My father's eyes dart to the gun behind me and I take a step to the right, keeping my arms out as Jules grips onto me. "Mason," she whispers desperately, her cries waning as she realizes there's still reason to be afraid. That this isn't over.

"Jules," I say although I stare straight ahead, keeping my eyes right where they belong. "He's the one who wrote the note. The one who set me up to meet your husband. He set Liam up and used all of us. All for a fucking payout."

All over a chunk of property in New York City that Anderson bought out from under him. One corrupt man upping the ante in a game he couldn't afford.

"Now, now, let's not get ahead of ourselves," my father says easily. "It wasn't meant to turn into this, Mason."

Jules releases me, letting out a gasp from behind me. I can't feel her, I can't see her, but I can't turn around. I have to keep my eyes on him. On the liar and murderer and sinner I was born from.

He raises his hands defensively, as if giving up the fight and says, "I swear to you, it wasn't supposed to end like this." All the lies, the spinning of a delicate web woven with manipulation and deceit.

"I don't believe you," I tell him. "I think you didn't care how many people had to be sacrificed."

The corner of his lips twist into a wry smile. "I certainly didn't intend for this, Mason." He shakes his head and adds, "Never."

"And Mom?" I ask, feeling the rage come back to me. Knowing this isn't the first time. I don't know how many lies he's told, or how many people he's killed. "Did you intend for her to die, or was she just a casualty of your games?"

The mention of my mother gets a rise from him, his eyes heating and his expression morphing into a snarl. "Your mother was a whore," he sneers. It's all I can take.

I heave in a breath as my body lunges for him. No punches, no hits. I wrap both of my hands around his throat. The weight of my body makes us topple over, both of us crashing to the ground as my blunt nails dig into the thin skin around his neck. I grip him with everything I have in me. My teeth clench and every muscle in my body is tight as I squeeze the life from him.

He tries to slam his fist into me at first, but he's not the young man he once was. I lean forward, balancing my weight as he tries to buck me off. I have him pinned.

Finally, he reaches up to his throat, desperate to pry away my fingers. His nails scratch at my skin, but I have no intention of letting go. All the desire in me focuses on leaning my weight into his throat. But the victory is stolen from me.

Bang! Bang!

My body tenses with the shock and fear. Two bullets have been fired. The noise rings in my ears as my father stills beneath me. His eyes are wide and lifeless, staring at nothing. His nails no longer digging into my hands.

Jules shot him. Once in the forehead, the other just an inch from his nose on his left cheek.

I stare at his face, the vision distorted by the blood dripping from the bullet holes down his weathered face and onto the carpet. Even knowing he's dead, I can't relax my grip around his throat.

Tell me! I scream in my head as tears prick the back of my eyes. I just want to hear him admit it. I want him to tell me to my face how he plotted my mother's death. How he hired someone to make it look like a suicide. My body trembles as I come to terms with the fact that it will never happen. His secrets will never be told, and my fingers loosen as I take in an unsteady breath.

It takes a long moment for me to glance up at Jules, who's eerily quiet only to see that she has the gun still pointed at him.

"He's dead. It's over, Jules."

Something in her seems to snap at my words, and she drops the gun as if it's burned her hands. She backs away, shaking and covering her mouth with horror.

The blood drains from her as the realization sets in. "Don't scream," I tell her.

"Look at me," I tell her and she does as I command. "It's okay." I swallow down every insecurity. For her, I'll be strong. I'll take care of this. "It's okay," I repeat and hold her gaze until she nods back although she's still on edge and drenched in terror.

I wipe the gun off on my shirt, getting rid of her prints and trying to think straight. The cops will be here soon. There's no doubt in my mind. She needs an alibi. "Run, Jules." I set the gun back down where it fell and rise to take a step closer to her. She's still trembling and can't take her eyes from the bodies on the ground. I reach out, grabbing her shoulders and shaking her slightly to get her attention. "Go to the Westin. You left me last night. Everyone knows that. I came here to get you, but you weren't here. I'll call the owner of the Westin." I nod as I speak, as if reassuring myself and her. I know for a fact the owner was in my father's back pocket and now he'll be in mine since I have my father's little black book. "He'll do what I tell him to if anyone asks. You checked in last night and that's where you've been."

Jules shakes her head, the implication of what I'm saying

setting in. "Mason," she says and sucks in a breath. "No. You can't."

"I can and I am," I tell her, staring deep into her eyes. My beautiful Jules, my sweetheart. I should have known it would end like this. It's how it should have started. With me killing my father and letting everything else go.

"I love you," I tell her, "even if you can't be with me. I love you."

She stares deep into my eyes, and I can see how much it tortures her. We were never meant to be. It was my mistake. I deserve this pain. She parts her lips, I'm sure to explain, I know her so well and I'm certain that's what's coming. But I don't need it. She doesn't have to explain it to me; I already know. I press my finger to her lips, silencing her and then giving her one last kiss.

She leans into me as I pull away and it makes the pain in my chest grow that much deeper. I look down at her with the tears soaking her lashes until she finally peeks up at me.

We share a look, but it only makes her cry harder. We both know it's over.

I hold her, wrapping my arms around her and kissing her hair until she's able to calm herself down. The clock is ticking, and the time we have is already up.

She gives me the saddest smile when I pull away again for the last time, and says, "You're always cleaning up my messes, aren't you?"

"It was never your mess, Jules." She can't stop the tears flowing freely down her face as I tell her, "I'm so fucking sorry." I drop her hand and take a step backward as she covers her face with her hand. I say, "Know that I'm sorry. Know that I love you."

She nods once, licking the tears from her lips as I tell her to go, listening to the sirens getting louder and louder.

I watch her disappear, and I don't regret it.

She needed me to let her go. I know that now. I'm only capable of destroying her. She deserves so much more than that.

twenty-eight

Julia

The truth is, everyone can kill.
Some born to defend, others for thrill.
What would it take? It's not that hard.
Threaten you? Or leave you scarred?
How much can they push you,
How much can they take?
Until you pull the trigger,
And you finally break.

I'VE NEVER HURT LIKE THIS BEFORE. LIKE MY SOUL'S been gutted.

I can't get the look in Mason's eyes out of my head.

A darkness sets in around me as I close my eyes. The vision of his handsome face displaying nothing but hopelessness is only replaced with something more morbid.

I killed a man. Two.

The first I could convince myself was an accident. I was terrified; I felt threatened. I swear it was an accident.

The second, though… I shot his father out of anger. I wonder if this is what Mason felt like almost a year ago when he killed Jace. If that rage that consumed me was the same for him. I shot his father because I wanted to. That is the only explanation.

I shift on the sofa and pull the chenille throw closer up to my neck. My shoulders brush against the armrest until I get my head right on the pillow. I can't go to the bedroom. I can't go anywhere in this hotel room without feeling like the cops will burst through the doors at any minute. I've only spoken to them on the phone. I can't imagine they believed my lies. Even as I said them, I could tell they sounded nothing like the truth. *Because I'm a liar now. I'm a murderer.*

I'm not the woman people think I am. I don't belong here and I don't deserve to get away without punishment. There's no denying that.

It's one thing to mourn the loss of a loved one. It's only natural, much like a breakup, but you have no way of going back, no way to mend the broken pieces. They simply don't exist anymore except in memories. Consuming your thoughts with no way to recover, other than to move on. Which, in itself, is a tragedy.

It's quite a different thing to mourn the loss of yourself. To realize you're no longer who you once were or who you wanted to be. Your identity has vanished, and staring back at you in the mirror is someone else entirely.

The faint sounds of the TV get louder as a commercial comes on and it makes my skin prick. I turn to face the lights, but I'm not watching it. I don't even know what's showing, it's all blurred. I wanted to turn something on to try to fill the hollowness in me. As if simply hearing something and someone else would make me feel less alone. As if I could somehow ignore my own reality by getting lost in a movie.

When Jace died, this method worked well. I'd turn on a heart-wrenching chick flick just to convince myself that the movie was the reason I was crying. The movie was why I felt the way I did and I could turn it off, if only I wanted to.

It's not working today, though. I'm all too aware of my current state. I bite down on my thumbnail, looking past the television and over at the curtains, hiding the view from the only window in the living room of the hotel penthouse.

I'm not the sweet good girl I was brought up to be.

And I never will be again. My stomach churns and I roll over to my side, trying to ignore the overwhelming guilt.

I try to convince myself that it'll be okay, that it was all a mistake or an accident or someone else's fault, but I've never been a good liar.

My throat dries and seems to close as I try to take a breath of air. It's all too much, this burden, this truth. Mostly the fact that I'm going to get away with it.

I wonder if Jace felt like this back when he sentenced that woman to death? I think back to each morning in his last days with me. But nothing was different. He was the same as any other day. The same smile, the same kiss. The same lightheartedness about him.

He had no remorse. I bite the inside of my cheek

wondering how he could go about his days as if everything was all right. Nothing is. And nothing has been for so long.

I can't hide that any longer. I can't run from it.

When did I become this woman? One willing to kill. Eager to, even.

I can't answer that, because I'd never been in this position until Jace died. All of my life, I've been handed everything easily. Even if I was grateful, it wasn't right.

I've never had to fight for a damn thing. I've never felt the need to defend myself. Maybe this woman, the one who kills out of anger, the one who's quick to end what threatens her... maybe I've always been her. I just didn't know it, because she was dormant deep down inside of me, comforted by the fact that she didn't need to act.

Life was kind to her, but not anymore.

My phone goes off by my thigh, making me jump as it rips me from my thoughts. Instinctively, I look to the door first. Where the cops should be coming any minute. They had to know I was the one who really did it. All the evidence is there in my home. *I should confess.*

They'll take me away and force me to pay for my crimes.

I'm expecting it. *I want it.* I want this all-consuming dread to leave me. I want the guilt to wash away. I want to be tried for my sins and sentenced as I should be.

Even if I sat on a jury and heard my story, I don't know how I'd find myself.

I'm guilty of so much, been baptized in the blood of other people's victims.

Maybe at this point, I'm insane. Maybe that will be my plea. It doesn't make me any less guilty.

I'm just as much of a murderer as Mason is.

And even more so than Jace, in a way.

I answer the phone on the last ring.

"Hello." I expect it to be the police, but it's Kat.

"Are you all right?" I close my eyes. It's good to hear her voice.

"How could I be?" I ask her with a pain she can't even imagine. She has no idea.

"It's going to be okay. I just got a call."

"From who?" I ask as I sit up straighter and pull my knees into my chest. "About Mason?" I need to know. "Is he going to be okay? Mason's going to be okay, is that what—"

"Calm down," she says, cutting me off. I sit uneasily, waiting for her to speak.

"What did you hear?"

She's quiet a second longer than I can stand. "He's in interrogation," she says. "They can charge him with obstruction now though, but that's it." My throat tightens and makes my words come out in a higher pitch than I intended.

"Obstruction?" I blink over and over, feeling light-headed.

Kat continues, "That's what I've heard. Nothing is set in stone yet."

My heart races erratically.

"It's not… I can't." I struggle to speak, to breathe even. "Kat, you have to help him. You have to help me." It's my chance to confess. To tell her everything. I throw my head back and I rock with the need to let it all out.

"It's okay, he didn't do it."

"I know he didn't. They can't keep him. They can't charge him with anything," I say, pleading with her as if I know how this all works. But I have no idea.

"Kat," I say as my voice cracks again and the words are right there, threatening to come out.

He's taking the fall for me, because he loves me.

And I'm letting him. God, it hurts. It's so wrong. I bury my face between my knees, hating my reality.

He said he loves me; he's taking the fall for me. I didn't even have the balls to tell him how I feel in return. He said I love you, and I said nothing. He must know. He has to. What we have is real and tangible. But I need to tell him.

"Is he going to get off?" I ask her and wait with bated breath. The other line is filled with the sound of her breathing deeply and I find myself hunching forward, my lungs squeezing with the need to breathe.

"Jules, they have some evidence."

Her words make my blood run cold. *Evidence?*

"He didn't do it," I say and the words leave me without my consent. I know they're from me, I know I said it, but I'm somewhere else. Not here, safe in a luxurious hotel penthouse while Mason sits in jail for a crime I committed.

"I know he didn't," she says and I'm not sure if she speaks with certainty for my benefit or if she really believes he didn't. She continues, "But for them to be holding him this long, it means they have something on him, Jules. Evan says they have something. There's something going on."

I swallow thickly, not responding as Kat repeats my name over and over again. The flashes of what happened haunt me. The blood, the heat, the kick of the gun in my hands.

"What can I do?" My voice is eerily calm as I stare straight ahead, although I see nothing but his father's lifeless eyes.

"There's nothing we can do, Jules," Kat says and I shake my head even though she can't see.

I could tell them everything.

"I'm coming over to the hotel," Kat says just as I say, "I'm going to the station."

"Why the hell would you do that?" she says as if it's absurd. "Don't you dare move.

"Trust me, Jules. Mason's going to get out of this. It's just a matter of time before we find out why he's still in holding." I run a hand through my hair, feeling desperate to do something.

"I can't just stay here," I tell her with the desperation apparent in my voice. "I have to do something."

"Not yet," she says. "Don't worry, he's going to be okay. I promise you. You need to stay where you are. Evan is going to keep his ear to the ground. I'll tell you everything as we know it. Right now, they could charge him with obstruction but they aren't… we're waiting to see what they have. Just wait."

My teeth pinch the inside of my cheek as I debate on waiting. It's what Mason told me to do too. I'm so tired of waiting. Waiting to feel again, waiting for the truth, waiting for vengeance, waiting for the guilt to leave.

"I can't—" I start to say but my voice cracks, and I close my eyes. I swallow before firming my resolve to tell Kat, but she cuts me off.

"Just wait one more day. They can't hold him more than that."

The guilt seeps into my veins as I nod my head once as I end the call. One day. One more day.

I learned to live without Jace. And I was better off for it.

I was happily living a lie. A false life that was devoid of real meaning.

I don't know that I can live without Mason, and I don't want to find out.

If I confess, we're apart.

If he takes the fall, we're apart.

I have to wait. I have no patience for fate. I don't know what's to come, but I won't let him do this.

As I walk to the large window watching the snow fall from the sky, I listen to the ticking of the clock, waiting to strike.

twenty-nine

Mason

"I DON'T HAVE ANYTHING ELSE TO SAY," I TELL the detective who's questioning me, the one who refuses to leave. The commissioner is across the room, waiting, eyeing me and probably wondering what his best move to make is. Now that my father's gone, the balance of power has shifted, so it's just a question as to where it's gone and how I play into this game.

Cracking my knuckles one by one, I watch as the skin tightens and turns white before settling into a bright red as I flex my hand.

I don't want anything to do with this shit. I never did, and I never will.

My eyes lift as Commissioner Haynes strides across the room, pulling out his chair slowly and letting the steel drag across the floor.

He leans back, crossing his arms and looking at me as if he's sizing me up. I'm sure this is an act, a game, something that he's done before. I merely look back to my hands. The ones I wrapped around my father's throat right before he died.

It's an odd sense of calm that washes over me at the thought. It shouldn't comfort me. It's not right to be grateful for another's death. I carried the weight and burden of Anderson's death for months. It was only after meeting Jules and knowing I could make her happy that made it all disappear. Maybe if I told her that, it would make it better, but I can't bring myself to do it. I don't want her to know how selfish I was.

I wish I could take it back. I wish I'd murdered my father instead. The rage was meant for him, it always was. I was too much of a coward to do it.

"We have the residue from your shirt, Thatcher." The commissioner finally speaks. I don't look up, I merely pick under my nails, ignoring him and the heat that makes every inch of my skin tingle. He leans across the table, moving closer to me with his hands clasped as he says matter-of-factly, "We know you didn't shoot him, but you're covering for someone. You wiped that gun clean."

Stupid. I grit my teeth, realizing just how stupid I was for doing that shit. I was so desperate to save her, I wasn't thinking. My heart pounds over and over again. But I don't show them a damn thing. I won't give them anything they can use against her.

It doesn't escape me that she could tell them everything. She could speak the truth and knowing my Jules, my sweetheart, I can see her doing it.

I could see her admitting it all, every last detail of the past year that's brought us to this moment. I'd still love her. I'd love her for it.

"I requested my lawyer," I remind them as I lift my head to look him in the eyes.

He clenches his jaw and the cop on my right shifts his stance, gaining my attention. He's pissed. He's young and naïve and thought he was going to break me. He thought that little bit of evidence would do something to scare me into talking.

But my father and grandfather taught me well. When the lies are too big to weave together, you stay silent. You wait for the right story to come along and slowly the pieces will snake in between the crevices. Those around you will create something that will hide them. Silence will kill the evidence. It only needs time.

"Your money can't save you this time," the young detective says. I don't even know his name, nor do I give a fuck. His dark eyes shine with conviction as he squares his shoulders and nods his head. He's clean-shaven, which only makes him appear younger, but of all the men I've met in this building, he's the only one I have respect for. He believes in justice.

"It never could," I speak without thinking, saying the first thing that came to mind.

"What's that mean?" Haynes questions from across the table. He's desperate for me to give him something.

I don't spare him a glance as the young cop responds, "You're going away. There's no negotiating, no lesser sentence for talking." His eyes narrow as he nods his head once and walks closer to the table, bracing himself on it with both of his fists. "We're going to find who really did it. And you're both going down."

My unaffected façade falters at the thought of them learning that Jules did it. My hands flex and ball into fists, and I have to look away. Not Jules. I already ruined her life enough. I destroyed a pure and beautiful soul.

Piece by piece I tore her down before I even knew what I was doing. I can't let her go down for this.

"Not talking is only making it worse for you."

I open my mouth to do what I do best, to be true to my heritage and lie. I have to think of something good, a reason for changing my shirt before cleaning the gun. I lick my lips, trying to come up with the right scenario, something believable. Something the evidence will prove is true. It doesn't have to be factual, only enough that will convince them I'm guilty.

This is what I deserve, even if it's a fucked-up way of going about it. I murdered a man. I tried and convicted him without thinking twice. It's only fair the same is done to me.

"Let's not get ahead of ourselves, Mickey," the commissioner says from across from me. "You already know that's not going to happen."

His last words catch my attention and I turn to him, ignoring how the detective's back straightens and he stalks toward Haynes. "Sir," the cop says and straightens, waiting for the commissioner to explain, maybe? I'm not sure. There's a duel between them with a thick tension that's suffocating.

The commissioner cocks a brow as if not understanding what Mickey is after.

"He's a witness, he tampered with the crime scene—"

"No judge is going to allow charges with that little evidence."

"Bullshit—"

"It's done," he says and the sharp words strike the young man, leaving him standing frozen, staring down the commissioner with his eyes flicking between the two of us. I don't know about legalities. I don't know how much is enough evidence. More importantly, I refuse to believe anything said by a man my father considered a friend.

"Find more evidence or let him go. It's that simple. We're not taking anything to trial unless we can ensure a conviction, get that through your head."

"You're as corrupt as they are," the detective says with contempt before turning his back to the commissioner and storming out of the room.

Before he can slam the door, I see a familiar face in the doorway, eyebrows raised as he's escorted in by a young female cop with a ponytail. She's looking between the cop who's just left and at Commissioner Haynes.

"I trust my client is free to go?" Mr. Millard asks as he shifts the leather handle of his black briefcase from one hand to the other and watches the female cop close the door to the room. "I'm sure you're aware—" Mr. Millard begins, but doesn't finish.

"I've already spoken to the judge," Commissioner Haynes says, once again leaning back in his chair and eyeing me, as if considering who I am and whether or not my existence even matters to him. "He's free to go," he says with finality as my family lawyer nods once and quickly reopens the door to the interrogation room. "We want the murderer and only him. Evidence proves Mason is not our suspect."

I don't need another invitation to leave. Standing abruptly, I take one last look at the commissioner, who's still staring straight ahead, but no longer at me. Only an empty chair, although the same look is in his eyes.

My pulse quickens as I walk through the station, feeling everyone's eyes on me and listening to the sound of our shoes smacking against the floor as we walk out.

"Just like that?" I say beneath my breath as Mr. Millard opens the large front glass door for me. His brow raises as I walk through, still looking at him and waiting for the other shoe to drop. For whatever deal was made and figuring out who I owe now.

He nods his head once, appearing uncomfortable but not adding any more.

This isn't the first time I've gotten away with things. A slap on the wrist for vandalism, shit like that. *But this?*

I stare at my lawyer, wondering what he knows and what he thinks of me as we leave, no charges pressed. The air is bitter cold and the snow on the street is blackened, but on the sidewalks it's still a brilliant white and makes the late evening seem lighter than it should.

"Just like that," Millard says, repeating my words and looking back over his shoulder before walking across the street. I follow him and wait. Always waiting for what's next.

He opens his car's passenger door and says, "Home, Mr. Thatcher?"

I shake my head no. A gust of wind blows by and the air seeps through my clothes, chilling me to the bone. Mr. Millard waits, as if expecting me to change my mind. But I'm not interested. I shake my head again, shoving my hands in my pockets.

My lawyer clears his throat and looks toward the station before shutting the door with a click and walking toward me. His oxford shoes crunch the snow beneath him as he leans in closer to me and says, "Don't tell anyone anything." He lets out a breath and it turns to fog in the air as he looks behind him one last time.

"It's going to take a couple of months for this to die down, of course. But the evidence found on the scene that could tie you to murder has been dismissed already. It's a matter of finding motive and suspects now. The judge is never going to charge a Thatcher, and he doesn't want any digging around the circumstances of your father's death." For the first time, Mr. Millard looks at me as if he thinks I may have done it, but there's no contempt, no disgust, only curiosity behind his eyes.

"For you, it's over. A few months, and it's all buried. Just stay quiet and don't talk to anyone. Don't give them a reason to come back to you. As far as they know, they followed you there, there was an altercation but a fourth unknown individual shot them both. Evidence proves you didn't fire a gun. They can't change that; they can only hunt down a fourth… and you have no idea of that person's identity. If anyone asks, you're only grateful he didn't shoot you too."

I nod my head, feeling the weight of everything and how it all seems heavier for some reason. Knowing how unjust it is. That a select few have already decided the fate of the case.

I'm a hypocrite, because it's what I did when I saw that look in Anderson's eyes. The smile on his face as I left his office. I did the same. His fate was sealed. Even a glance at the photograph on his desk didn't stop me.

I saw her. I knew he was married. I knew she was his. I

told myself I didn't care and that it didn't matter. He had to die.

It's that overwhelming feeling of power that made the first domino tip as I turned my back on him, knowing his fate was decided.

"Thank you, Mr. Millard," I say and turn away from the station, away from him and toward the crowded streets of the city.

I didn't know how the other dominoes would fall. And the judge and the lawyers, they have no idea either. So many pieces tumbled over. So many lives affected.

There's only one who matters to me.

Only one I need to keep safe.

Her piece is bound to fall if I touch her. I almost ruined her once. I won't do it again.

I was never any good for her. I should have stayed away if I loved her, and I think I did even all that time ago. I think I loved her before I ever heard that sweet laugh. Before I saw her gorgeous lips and that sadness in her beautiful doe eyes that she hid from everyone but me. I think I loved her even then.

And I should have stayed far away.

thirty

Julia

They say if you love someone, you should let them go.

That's all I keep thinking over and over as I stare out the windows of the penthouse, staring blankly at the city skyline. Mason's been out for over twenty-four hours now. I knew the second he walked out, and I waited. And waited. I owe him and all I can think is that if I send him a message, I'm going to beg him for even more. That's not fair and that's not right.

I swallow thickly, and my dry throat sends a spike of pain running through me. Or maybe it's my heart. I'm not sure which. I shake my head, turning abruptly and walk over to the kitchen to fix myself some coffee. If he wanted to speak to me, he would have come or he would have called. The fact is, he doesn't want me. Why did it take me this long to realize that wanting him and loving him wasn't enough?

He hasn't called, hasn't sent a text. I take a steadying breath, balancing myself on a padded barstool at the island counter and then gripping the hot mug of coffee with both hands. The ceramic mug has veins of gold running through the thick cream pottery. I focus on it and drift my finger over the raised texture remembering how he used to trail his fingers down my lips before kissing me.

Everything is a reminder of him and it hurts. I let my head fall back to exhale before taking a slow sip of the coffee. It's worse than death because I could have him. It could be different… He's right there.

I keep thinking he's merely let me go because he loves me. They say if you love someone, you should let them go. Maybe that's what I should do. I should let him go.

But isn't it done with? Isn't it over? The ending is so much different from what I envisioned. I will take this one where there is hope, over anything else. I want a chance.

The truth is, if Mason loved me, he'd be here. If he wanted me, he'd take me. That's the kind of man he is.

"If you want to go to his house…" Maddie says gently from the seat next to me, moving her hand to my thigh. She hasn't left my side since last night when the girls came over. When Kat told me Mason had been released from custody and I had waited for him to show, and he never did. After the first hour, I started to worry. After several hours, it was hard not to assume the worst. I'm glad my friends were here with me instead. I still don't know when I'll be able to return to my condo. The police say it's a crime scene, and that means it's off-limits in the meantime. I should message him… I should message Mason and let him know that. Shouldn't I? He should know that I'm still here in this penthouse when he's the one who's footing the bill.

"Maddie, please." Kat's patience is waning thin with a restless Maddie who won't stop asking questions. I'm grateful for the distraction, though.

Kat's sitting at the dining room table and Sue went to work. She didn't want to, but I insisted.

"There's nothing wrong with going after what you want," Maddie says, finishing her suggestion.

I glance from her to Kat, who's gently nodding her head. "That's true," she whispers. Both of them stare at me as if I'm broken. Like this is the one thing over the last year that has managed to finally destroy me.

I've lost a husband, then fell in love with his murderer. I've been held against my will, killed a man out of anger and another out of fear for my life.

Yet here I sit, worried about the man who brought all of this chaos in my life.

Worried he doesn't want me. Worried I can never have him again. Worried I'll never love anyone or be loved by anyone like him.

The mug clinks as I set it down on the counter, pushing it away to rest my face in my hands. The granite's cold on my elbows, but everything today has been brutally cold. I should be used to it by now.

Shifting on the stool next to me, Maddie gently rubs my back in soothing strokes, making the cotton blouse travel slightly up and down my back as she shushes me.

The padding of Kat's feet are muted by her socks when she gets up to sit by us too. She takes a seat alongside us at the island with me sitting between her and Maddie.

"Hey, it's okay. He didn't do it," Kat says in such a tender voice. It only makes the pain in my chest grow.

I didn't tell them a word, and I never will. They'll never know any of this truth. Not if I can help it.

"I know," I say and my voice cracks as I agree. I clear my throat and stare straight ahead, pushing the hair out of my face and ignoring both sets of their questioning eyes on me.

I can see myself in the reflection of the steel fridge, but it's not quite me, it's something else. Some different version that stares back, distorted. Perception is what's changed my life. It could have gone on and on with me not knowing a damn thing, only seeing what they wanted me to, and then none of this would have ever happened.

"He didn't do it," I say in a stronger voice, swallowing the lump in my throat.

"Why don't you call him maybe?" Maddie offers.

I have to drop my gaze. I can't look them in the eyes and lie. "I don't think he wants me to," I answer honestly, staring fixedly at the granite countertops.

"You're wrong, Jules." Kat's voice comes out harsher than I expected as she speaks, and I grip the edge of the counter to turn my body on the stool and face her. "Of course he loves you. That's more than obvious."

"You don't understand," I tell her even though I already know there's no convincing her. Kat's stubborn. She stares at me, waiting for an explanation. My eyes flicker to Maddie's, both of them waiting impatiently. I settle for a partial truth. "He said he loves me." I clear my throat and look past Kat. "I didn't say it back," I add. "The last time I saw him, I didn't say it back."

"Why?" Maddie sounds horrified, and it only makes me feel worse.

"It's just that he did something," I say haltingly, and my stomach churns as I look back to the gold flecks on the mug in front of me.

"Something like what?" Kat seems hesitant.

"It was something from a while ago, but it hurt me," I say then close my eyes, wishing they could just know. Wishing I didn't have to say it for them to understand.

"Did he mean to hurt you?" Kat asks and there's a pain in her gaze. I know it's because of what she and Evan are going through right now. I wish she'd talk to me about that, rather than feeling like I'm prying when I try to ask how she's holding up.

"I'm sure he didn't," Maddie says softly, but her brow is furrowed with sympathy as she waits for my response.

"It wasn't meant to, no, but it was meant to hurt someone else and it wasn't right." I see Maddie and Kat exchange glances.

"What did he do?" Maddie asks.

"Maybe he's not here because he thinks you want to keep your distance for now since he was arrested?" Kat says, delicately hinting around the fact that I'm very self-conscious of negative publicity.

"I don't care about that," I tell her bluntly. "He's not here now, because when I left…" I can't finish. I can't say the words because I'm ashamed that I didn't answer him. I've known I still love him. I know damn well I do, and I did then. I just didn't want to admit it.

"You upset him?" Kat says, taking a guess.

"I knew I might not see him again… and I still didn't say it back. He said I love you, and I didn't say it back."

"It's just words," Kat says, "Actions are what count. And if you love him, go for him. Fix it. You can always fix it." She's full of so much confidence. So much conviction, I have to believe her although part of me wonders if she's telling me what she's telling herself when it comes to her own relationship.

"Go to him," Maddie says sweetly.

"Don't you want him?" Kat presses when I don't respond, too caught up in my own thoughts.

Had I known the truth, I never would have gotten close, but he didn't give me that chance. He pulled me in and drowned me before I realized I couldn't breathe. I'll forever be his. All the sins and secrets could never tear us apart. We both have them. But if we have each other… they don't matter.

Maddie nods her head in agreement. "Just because you're fighting over something that happened before this doesn't mean anything." Her voice is firm. "He needs you."

And I need him. We always have, both in our own way.

All three of us turn our heads to the door as I hear it open with a loud thud. My heart hammers in my chest, pounding harder and harder as I see him. Mason.

The breath leaves my lungs and I nearly fall off the stool at the sight of him.

He doesn't look at me or even in this direction as he closes the door and tucks the keycard into his pocket. He slips off his boots easily, as if he belongs here and it's only natural.

As if he hadn't kept me waiting here for him for hours.

When he finally looks up, something breaks in me. The walls crumble, and I want to run to him. To climb off the stool and embrace him.

To thank him for taking the fall. For protecting me. For loving me even if he brought all this hell along with him. To check him over and make sure he's okay.

But I'm frozen in place. Paralyzed by the sight of him. He rolls his broad shoulders before tossing the jacket over the sofa and finally looking up at me. His steel gray eyes pierce through me, questioning only for a moment before turning his attention to the other two women.

Kat's hand squeezes mine briefly before she whispers, "Do you want us to get out of here?"

"Yeah," Maddie answers for me. "We'll see you tomorrow?" Maddie asks with wide eyes.

I nod my head, but still I can't speak. I can't answer either of them. He's here. All I can do is be thankful that he's here.

He's standing right there, only inches away from me. I can still feel the coldness from the outdoors around him. But it doesn't belong to him in the least. His tanned skin is pink on his cheeks and the tip of his nose. My fingers itch to reach out to him, to touch him and pass the chill of the air and feel his hot skin.

I'm vaguely aware of Kat and Maddie leaving, the sounds of keys jingling and each saying hello and then good-bye to Mason.

He gives them a tight smile and nods, his deep voice sending a soothing wave through me as he shoves his hands in his pockets and watches them leave.

As soon as the door shuts, he looks back at me,

consuming me the way he does with his full attention as comes to the bar, close to me. Close enough to touch.

I lick my lips and scoot forward on the stool, my left knee brushing his right. "Mason," I say, whispering his name with a reverence I'm not sure he hears or recognizes, but his eyes look the same way they did months ago when I first left him. Raw and vulnerable. Emotional.

He can hide a lot of things from me, and I won't deny that because it's the absolute truth. But I can see the pain and love in his gaze when he looks at me like this.

I know that's real. He can't ever hide that from me.

"Jules," he says and Mason's voice is low. Too low. Panic drifts into my veins. It courses through me as he reaches out to run his fingers down my hair before resting his large hand on my thigh. His thumb runs back and forth in soothing strokes, but there's something about the way he's looking at me, something off about his body language. Something I don't like.

"I never should have put you through all this, Jules."

My heart clenches, feeling so constricted that I can't fathom the amount of pain I'm feeling. He's letting me go. He gave me hope, walking through the door. *No! No! Go back to the hope. We have hope. We don't have everything but we have hope, don't we?* The words tangle over themselves in the back of my throat.

"I never should have," he says then swallows before continuing, "I never should have killed him. I'm sorry." All I can do is shake my head slightly as I listen to Mason. It was a mistake, an unforgivable sin. An act that ruined my life. But he had his reasons. I can't deny that it was wrong, but so much was wrong. The pieces fell, and there was blood on everyone's hands.

"I was a different man then. I didn't know you yet, and I can't ever take it back." Mason pulls his hand away, and the warmth and comfort of his touch vanishes, replaced by a sudden chill.

"I fell in love with you and I'd do anything to keep you, but I know you don't want that.

I hate myself as much as you hate me."

He starts to turn away from me. To leave me like I've wanted since I learned the truth, but my body comes to life, my blood a mix of anxiety and depression. I grip Mason's hand as I stumble off the stool, the damn thing nearly toppling over.

"Don't you dare leave me," I say. My voice comes out raw as tears threaten to spill from my eyes. I refuse to take my hands from his to wipe under my eyes.

Never.

He's as much mine as I am his. I refuse to let him go.

His expression changes as he registers my words. "Don't you ever leave me again," I tell him with a strength formed from panic. *Please, please God, don't let him deny me.*

"I need you." The hot tears fall to my lips and I try to swallow, but it hurts too much. Everything hurts as I stand before the man I love, knowing it's wrong. Knowing he broke me, ruined me and then showed me how fucked up love can be. The only cruel thing left for him to do to me would be to leave me like this. To throw me away after everything we've been through.

"There's hope, isn't there?" I say. "I love you," I whisper with complete conviction.

Just as I part my lips to confess every emotion in me to him, he crashes his lips against mine, filling my chest with a warm flow of desire and completion. My lips are hard at first, caught off guard, but I'm quick to mold them to his, spearing my fingers through his hair as his hand splays at the small of my back, both of us deepening the kiss, both of us wanting more.

"Mason." I moan his name as he breaks the kiss, my eyes still closed as our hot breath mingles between us.

"Just hold me. I love you," I tell him and bury my head into his hard chest. He wraps his strong arms around me as his warmth consumes me and kisses my hair over and over. This is where I belong, I know it is.

"I love you," he says and it's all I need.

I love Mason. And he loves me.

epilogue

Julia

Deceit is pretty,
The truth is better than the lie.
Its beauty lurks in darkness,
It's gorgeous in ways you can't deny.

Although the tale is strange,
Not the ever after for you and me.
It's broken and imperfect,
And the way fate meant it to be.

Y BRUNETTE HAIR LOOKS NEARLY BLACK WHEN it's wet. The brush makes a loud thud as I set it down and reach for my makeup bag.

Looks can be so deceiving, can't they?

We have a beautiful home, seemingly the perfect life and many days, that's all I see. It's all I saw with Jace too, but that was a sham and a lie and I realize now that I knew the truth well back then. I was happy with the image, but the truth was something I hid; I wanted it that way.

What I have with Mason is the opposite. Although no one can see the truth, I know what we are. Raw and broken, but together, we're whole.

The world will never know what it took for the two of us to come out of this alive. No one will ever realize how much strength there is between us. We're unbreakable. Shattered to pieces, but healed together with a scar that's so much stronger than what was once there.

It's not a fairytale, but it's a happily ever after suited for us both. It gives me chills when I look back at the past, but I don't do that often. It's much better to look ahead, at the true happiness and comfort we give each other. At the full life of trust and faith that's been forged between us.

My phone pings with another text from Kat. And then another.

She finally told me what's happening with her and Evan.

He's still your Evan, I answer and stare at my phone, waiting for her response.

If anyone ever heard my story, maybe they'd say what I did was wrong. That crawling back to Mason after knowing what he did, is simply unforgivable.

Even my closest friends. I don't think they would understand. No one would.

Love is inexplicable. It makes you do crazy things. Love is blind… that's a saying for a reason, isn't it?

I know, Kat writes back. *He's still the man I married. Dangerous in ways I don't like to think about. I did this to myself. I knew better than to fall for him.*

My heart hurts for her when she messages again before I can respond: *I only wish love were enough to fix this…*

It is. I'm desperate to write that back to her. But there are pieces to their story I'm missing. Pieces that will come out one way or another…

ABOUT THE
author

Thank you so much for reading my romances. I'm just a stay at home mom and avid reader turned author and I couldn't be happier.

I hope you love my books as much as I do!

More by Willow Winters
www.WillowWintersWrites.com/books